ANDRE GONZALEZ

Zero Hour

For my grandpa, Pete.

"Time is a storm in which we are all lost."

-William Carlos Williams

Contents

GET EXCLUSIVE BONUS STORIES!

Connecting with readers is the best part of this job. Releasing a book into the world is a truly frightening moment every time it happens! Hearing your feedback, whether good or bad, goes a long in shaping future projects and helping me grow as a writer. I also like to take readers behind the scenes on occasion and share what is happening in my wild world of writing. If you're interested, please consider joining my mailing list. If you do so, I'll send you the following as a thank you:

1. A free copy of *Revolution*, a prequel story that goes back in time before Chris Speidel ever knew about the mysterious world of time travel.
2. A free copy of *Road Runners*, a prequel story that visits the origination of the Road Runners organization.

You can get your content **for free,** by signing up HERE.
https://www.andregonzalez.net/Wealth-Of-Time-Bonus

1

Chapter 1

Martin Briar could resist the freezing of time, but that didn't stop his life from coming to a standstill. The world of time travel—and more importantly, the Road Runners—was set to undergo the grandest changes of its existence.

Never had a commander been assassinated. Never had a fresh recruit joined the Road Runners and made a run for the commandership. And never had a Keeper of Time guarded their power so stingily and gone into hiding while the world virtually crumbled.

Chris Speidel had divided the time travelers, pitting all members against each other like pawns in some sick chess match that he oversaw. Trust had been broken, lifelong peaceful relationships vanishing within a few years of his reign, clearing the path for him to run the world of time travel as an unchecked dictator.

Tonight, however, none of that mattered. At least for the time being.

Martin sat in one of the Denver office's small conference rooms with his campaign manager—rather, Commander

Blair's campaign manager—Tony Jenkins, each man puffing a cigar and blowing clouds of smoke that filled the cramped room.

"It's crazy how fast it goes, isn't it?" Tony asked through the haze. They sat around a small square table in the only two chairs available in the meeting space. "When you start the campaign, Election Night seems a hundred years away. Then before you know it, here we are, less than an hour from hearing the results."

"I can't believe it." Martin hadn't smoked a cigar since the last time he tried to pull the trigger on himself at his old apartment in Larkwood. He closed his eyes and imagined the view from that old balcony, the mountains grand in the distance, the skies a crisp, never-ending blue. And the ashtray that deemed him the world's greatest father, oftentimes catching tears along with the spent ash he flicked into it.

What the hell has happened to my life? he wondered. If the time from campaigning to election night was one hundred years, then this particular moment on the balcony was at least a *million* years in the past.

Martin spent most nights staring in the mirror, trying to remember what life had been like before he accepted that pill from Chris in the Wealth of Time antique store. It almost seemed that the old Martin had died and a newer version was born in the reincarnate. He could hardly remember anything from his past. Except for the *pain*. The pain stuck like tree sap on a windshield.

"Whatever happens tonight, you've sparked a movement," Tony continued.

"A movement? Or more division within the organization?" Martin asked, shrugging his shoulders.

2

"The division isn't what you think. Yes, people are scared out of their minds and want to forget all of this, but in time they'll realize that we eventually need to crawl out of the shadows and move forward."

An unexpected candidate emerged in the race for the commandership. A gentleman named Yohan Templeton ran a platform based on cowardice, vowing to help the Road Runners remain in hiding, and even went as far as promising them protection in a remote location where no Revolters could ever find them.

His ideology was so absurd that no one took him seriously at first. But within a three-week time span and thousands of TV and radio commercials, he formed a massive following, ready to trade in their lives as time travelers and live in euphoria wherever this faux, remote location existed.

Yohan was sleazy, especially for the Road Runners who had never seen a candidate spew constant slander about his opponents and run a campaign with promises that rivaled those of middle school class elections. Apparently, the membership let fear control their logic, and they actually bought into his nonsense, creating a rougher road to the commandership for Martin than originally expected.

"I just don't understand how Yohan has even made this a race," Martin said, taking a puff of the cigar nearing its end. "I expected a fight—hell, I expected to lose—but not to someone like *this*. Surely there was going to be a smart, experienced candidate with all the answers to our problems who would best me at the polls. Instead it's come down to me and this clown."

Tony shook his head. "He stroked people's fears. His ads are all a reminder of what happened to Strike, to the Council, to their own friends and family now living under a rock. It's been

3

weeks of constantly mounting fear, where he presents himself as the safety net. Frightening, yes – but a brilliant campaign."

Martin didn't appreciate the compliment, but held his tongue. After spending the last several weeks on the road, meeting Road Runners from the Arctic Circle, to the hills of Panama, and everywhere in between, the last thing Martin wanted to hear was a vote of confidence toward his opponent out of the lips of his own campaign manager.

"Look, Martin, if things turn out for the worse, you have a place to stay in England with me."

"So I can run into hiding just like Yohan wants? I appreciate the offer, but that would look absolutely absurd after ranting for six weeks about digging our feet in and fighting the Revolution."

"I suppose that's true, but just know the offer always stands. Sometimes matters can spin beyond our control and leave you with no option *but* to run."

A knock banged on the door and Martin's stomach immediately clenched into a knot. Tony put out his cigar in the ash tray. "Looks like it's time."

Tony had instructed someone come get them once the news broadcast was ready to read the results of the election. The moment of truth now waited on the other side of the door where an office full of faithful Road Runners watched in anticipation to know what the future held for their organization. Tony rose as Martin finished his cigar and joined him, opening the door to a room full of two dozen pairs of anxious eyes that followed them down the long hallway until they gathered with the rest of the office watching the big-screen TV.

"What's the word?" Tony asked. The TV showed a campaign ad of Yohan walking through a tranquil park, welcoming all

Road Runners to join him in a new world of peace.

"They'll have the results after the commercials," Lila Lawson said. She had worked tirelessly for the campaign over the past four weeks, and it showed in the form of bags under her eyes, her light brown hair a frazzled mess.

Life had slowly returned to normal for a fraction of the Road Runners. Election season raised spirits and brought hope for many who had been in hiding. The Denver office was currently filled with four members of the campaign team sent by Commander Blair. The other twenty people were local Road Runners who wanted to join the cause and help spread the word of Martin Briar to lead them all out of the darkness.

Many prominent Road Runner figures remained in hiding, however. The Council had still yet to show their faces. Their highly-popular news broadcaster, Chip Halsey, who had resigned on live television after Strike's public execution, had yet to turn up.

Regardless, Road Runners were ready for the next chapters of their lives and grouped together for a smoothly-run election. While the Council typically orchestrated the election and counting of results, a group of volunteers with members from all countries in North America worked to run the election process. A new broadcaster stepped into the role, a young woman who refused to hold back her passion when discussing the future of the organization and brought a sense of urgency to her viewers. The culture had definitely changed, but the dread that had loomed over them since the disappearance of the Council had slowly started to fizzle out.

Blaring trumpets whined from the TV, grabbing everyone's attention as the office fell silent. A middle-aged woman with black hair, dark skin, and sparkling brown eyes filled the screen.

"Ladies and gentlemen, thank you for joining me tonight. Welcome to all returning viewers, and for those of you who are tuning in for the first time, my name is Jennifer Rodriguez."

Jennifer held a white envelope in her trembling hands. "Here I have the results for our special election for the commander-ship. This is perhaps the most important election of our lives, and I can only hope we have made the correct decision as an organization. If you've watched all day, you'll know the survey calls were too close to conclude a result."

The voting software sent surveys to random voters through-out the day in an attempt to learn any particular voting trends while the results poured in. These surveys showed a split decision, Martin and Yohan each with forty-two percent of the votes, the other sixteen percent going to other candidates in the race. A simple majority was needed to win the election.

From the onset, Tony had projected forty-six percent of the votes would be needed to claim victory, yet neither candidate ever approached that mark through the thousands of voluntary surveys returned.

"It's time for us to learn the results of our future," Jennifer said. She thumbed open the envelope, an action that seemed to drag on for ten minutes as Martin and the rest of the Denver office watched with their collective breaths held.

She finally opened it and unfolded the sheet of paper within, sliding on a pair of reading glasses as her eyes pored over the paper. Jennifer kept her lips pursed until she looked up to the camera and into the souls of Road Runners watching around the world.

"With a majority of the votes at forty-five percent, it is my pleasure to announce the next commander of the Road Runners as Martin Briar."

6

Jennifer's lips kept moving, but her words were drowned out as the office erupted in cheers and applause. High fives, hugs, and handshakes went all around, while some stood there clapping with their eyes bulging at the TV. Martin's heart froze as he gawked at the screen, Jennifer replaced by an image of his own face, the banner reading as: *Commander Martin Briar to be sworn in tomorrow.*

"Holy shit, mate," Tony said, sticking out a hand to shake. "We did it. *You* did it."

Martin shook his hand, yet remained speechless. The whole thing felt surreal, like a dream he'd surely wake up from in the coming moments. The others in the office made their rounds, eventually reaching Martin who had just become the most prominent figure within the entire organization. He accepted hugs and handshakes from those who had dedicated their lives to his campaign over the past month, his jaw hanging open in between the quick words of thanks he returned.

There's no way this is happening, he thought, again the memories of his past life being pushed further back like a forgotten toy under a child's bed. The weight of responsibility had yet to strike him, and would remain on hold until he truly sat down to get to work.

His cell phone buzzed uncontrollably in his pocket, flooded with text messages of congratulations from the many people he had formed relationships with all around the continent.

The vibrations changed pace to signify an incoming phone call, prompting Martin to pull out his phone to see his new lieutenant commander on the caller ID. He answered the call and cupped a hand over his mouth to block the cacophony of celebration in the background.

"Gerald," Martin greeted. "How are you, good sir?"

7

"I'm doing great, *Commander.*"

Martin had never heard such joy in Gerald's voice.

"I can't believe this is happening," Martin said, turning his back away from a group of Road Runners who were hollering over a popped champagne bottle spraying liquid all over the office.

"It happened. I just wanted to give a quick call to congratulate you. I look forward to moving out to Denver and getting started. We have lots to do." Gerald had left the year 2064, but remained in his hometown Chicago while he adjusted to life in 2020. Now, he'd be packing up his life to live in Denver for the next two years while serving as the lieutenant commander. "I'll let you get back to the party. Have a good night and I'll see you tomorrow afternoon."

"Thanks, Gerald, see you then."

Martin hung up and felt a bit more in control of himself as reality had started to settle in. The mood in the office had completely shifted to upbeat after weeks of stress and fatigue. Someone handed Martin a glass filled with champagne and he promptly gulped it, the suds burning his throat on their way down.

He had kept his cell phone in hand, and glanced down when it vibrated once more. On the screen was a text message from Chris Speidel: *Congrats, friend. I look forward to dancing with you 'til the end.*

Suddenly, Martin no longer felt like celebrating.

2

Chapter 2

Martin woke the next morning in the office that once belonged to Tarik Sadi, the former Lead Runner of the Denver chapter who had fled during the pandemonium. The room would soon expand with the knocking down of a couple walls, and transform into the office of a commander, equipped with special security measures, a pantry of non-perishable foods, and several other functions that the leader of the Road Runners required.

Construction would take a couple weeks to complete, but Martin still slept in the pullout bed and planned to do so for the coming weeks. A crew would also start work on his house in Littleton to beef up the security by installing bulletproof windows, cameras and sensors, a new lock system on all doors, and converting the basement into an official command center and panic room.

Martin had no involvement in the process, most of the Denver team working on both projects simultaneously. His time was now exclusive to serving the Road Runners, any other detail of life to be taken care of by his eager staff.

Commander Blair was scheduled to arrive in Denver at ten o'clock to swear in Martin as the new commander, a task typically performed by the Council. Later that afternoon, Gerald would show up to start his new life as the number two in charge, the rest of the day set aside for him and Martin to discuss their upcoming plans for their two-year term as the new leaders.

Once dressed and ready for the day, Martin stepped out to the bullpen, many of his staff still snoozing after a long night of celebrating. They had worked tirelessly for weeks, and he saw no issue in letting everyone cut loose to balance it out.

"Good morning, Commander Briar," Tony greeted from a nearby desk, a steaming mug of coffee held to his lips. "Ready for your first day?"

"Sure am," Martin said. "Did you get some rest last night?"

"Oh, I'm fine," Tony said with a smirk. "I had one drink then went to bed. My days of all-nighters are well behind me. Commander Blair left London early and should be getting here in about a half hour."

Martin checked his watch to see it was already 8:30. His stomach growled for breakfast. "I'm going to eat before he gets here. Can you start waking everyone up to get ready?"

"Absolutely."

Martin had just given his first order and loved the feeling. He had no intent on becoming a bossy asshole, but it was nice that if he needed something done, all he had to do was say so.

He grinned and nodded to Tony before heading toward the kitchen to find something to eat.

* * *

Commander Blair arrived at the office at 9:15, security surrounding him in the form of men and women dressed in black suits, guns surely concealed underneath their blazers. Tony greeted him at the entrance and the two caught up for a few minutes until Martin came out of his office.

"Commander Martin Briar," Blair said with a wide smile. "Welcome to the club."

"Thank you for everything," Martin said, sticking out a hand to shake, Blair waving it away and moving in to hug Martin with a slap on the back.

"I simply provided resources. *You* won over the people. Shall we get started, though? It's not good to leave a commander not sworn in for any longer than necessary."

Martin nodded. "I believe the big conference room is set up for us."

Everyone who had been sleeping in the bullpen had already made their way to the conference room, where a podium had been staged along with the cameras to broadcast the event for all Road Runners to see.

A handful of stragglers joined the two commanders as they walked down the hallway.

The conference room had rows of seats facing the podium, all filled with the familiar faces of those who worked to get him elected. Commander Blair swiftly made his way to the podium, stopping to hug a few people he had known in the audience.

"Mic check," he said, the chatter in the room falling silent as all eyes looked ahead. "Cameras good?"

The camera operator gave a thumbs up.

"Mr. Briar, please join me at the front of the room. Go ahead and roll the cameras."

The camera operator nodded and pushed a button on the

device. The pre-show countdown began as Blair gripped the sides of the podium, Martin's eyes drawn to his hairy knuckles. The light on the camera turned green and he started speaking.

"Good morning, fellow Road Runners. For those of you who don't know me, I am Commander Blair from Europe. I'm here today to swear in North America's newest commander.

"I want to first thank you all for voting in this special election. It's never easy to replace someone as beloved as Commander Strike, but you all rose to the occasion with the highest voter turnout in your continent's history. Ninety-six percent of the population voted, an astronomical number compared to prior elections."

The small crowd offered a round of applause, giving Blair a chance to swig from the glass of water placed on the podium's lower shelf.

"I'm joined up here with Martin Briar, last night's winner in what was a very close race. Mr. Briar, will you please turn and face me?"

Martin obliged, feeling all eyes in the world on him.

"Thank you. Please place your left hand behind your back and raise your right hand."

Martin did as instructed, his hand slightly quivering as the anticipation brewed a storm within.

"Do you, Martin Briar, vow to lead the North American Road Runners in times of stress and times of peace?"

"I do."

"Do you vow to protect the organization by any means possible from all threats, internal or foreign?"

"I do."

"Will you seek an end to the war against the Revolution, whether through force or diplomacy?"

"I will."

"Do you vow to preserve, protect, and defend the integrity of this organization, starting on this day, and every day after?"

"I do."

"Should you ever deem yourself unfit to hold the position of commander—whether it be mentally, emotionally, or physically—will you inform the appropriate parties to execute a peaceful transition of power to your Lieutenant Commander?"

"I will."

Blair grinned and clasped his hands. "Ladies and gentlemen of the North American Road Runners, it is my distinct privilege to officially introduce for the first time Commander Martin Briar."

The small crowd erupted, creating much more noise than expected for a couple dozen people. Both commanders stood behind the podium, grins wide, and hands clenched in a definitive shake. A couple of photographers started snapping pictures, capturing a photo that Martin planned to hang on his office wall for the entirety of his commandership.

"Now the fun begins," Blair said under his breath as they held their pose for a few more seconds. "Do you have a minute to chat when this is all done? In private?"

Martin nodded, holding his grin for the cameras where they'd remain for another ten minutes.

* * *

The two commanders returned to Martin's office that would soon undergo its transformation.

"How do you feel?" Blair asked, taking the seat across Martin's desk.

Martin raised his eyebrows and tossed his hands. "Stunned. Like maybe I'm walking through some sort of trippy dream."

Blair chuckled. "It's funny how you never hear that sentiment from prominent figures in the world—they all pretend it's a normal part of life. But we all go through that same reluctance to believe it's all real."

"I'm sure it'll feel normal in time, but last night and today have just been surreal."

"I emailed you some information—all the boring work that needs to be done right after you're sworn in. You have to hire a staff for all sorts of roles. Gerald will also need to do most of these tasks for his direct team. As you know, the new commander doesn't give a big speech until a week after the swearing in. You'll need to prepare that speech—or hire some writers to do it for you."

"So I'm just hiring a bunch of people to do stuff for me? What do I actually do?"

"Once your staff is in place, you'll get to focus on your agenda. Aside from that, you're sure to have a heap of decisions to make on a daily basis. Remember, you're the *commander* – all requests for mission specific time-travel must come through your office."

"Is there a reason I'd ever decline someone's request?"

Blair scoffed at the question. "Well, yes, that's the point. I decline about a dozen requests each day. People make requests for no good reason, or for things too ambitious. Your main considerations are keeping our members safe, and keeping our existence a secret. You need to weigh many factors with each request that'll be outlined in each application. For example, suppose a person of color requests to go on a mission to Alabama in the early 1800's. Not a wise choice."

"Why would someone do that?"

"You'd be surprised. I probably get one application each week from a Jewish member requesting to go to 1940's Germany. It's always an emotional request. They want to go back to try and save their ancestors. So, it's both dangerous and meaningless—an easy decline."

"But I've traveled around time without ever requesting permission."

"Anyone can travel wherever they want, at their own risk. A *mission* will assist the member in the forms of additional Road Runners, weaponry, and strategy. Like when you went into the future for the Alzheimer's medicine. Having that medicine would have benefited the Road Runners, so it was accepted and you were given a whole team to travel with. People understand the risk if they travel on their own—there are too many of us to truly keep a tab on everyone's activity, although we do try."

"And it's my sole decision if someone's request is deemed worthy?"

Blair nodded. "Either you or Gerald can make those calls—no one else. I consider if the request helps the organization in any way, and I try to keep it that simple."

"Alright, that seems reasonable."

"Now, you'll have all week to worry about these things. I want to know, before I go back, what's on your early agenda?"

"Well, I'd like to restore order and structure here. I'm going to make a call for our Council members to return to their job. And if they don't, I'll be replacing them with fresh blood."

"I love it."

"Once the Council is in place, all focus shifts to Chris and figuring out how to get rid of him. I don't suppose there's a way to get any support from you guys in Europe?"

"Afraid not. Since Chris has never been deemed a threat in Europe, we have no right to interfere."

"That's so ridiculous."

"I agree it is, for this scenario. But our founders believed that all continents remain separate and not interfere with each other. We all have different ideas of what is dangerous, and in turn, different approaches on how to deal with threats. If Chris was in South America, he'd have been wiped off the map by now. They're ruthless down there, but none of that is the point."

"Well, that's why I chose Gerald. The man is a genius. You should've seen the way he navigated us through the future. I can't say that I ever truly felt in danger, even though I should have. He'll be here this afternoon if you want to hang around."

"Afraid I need to get going in the next few minutes—I've got my own continent to run."

Blair winked across the desk as he rose to his feet.

"Understood," Martin said. "I assume we'll be in touch a lot more often now?"

"Certainly. Even though we can't interfere with each other, we do talk things over and have pretty meaningful discussions. At the end of the day, we're all just trying to keep our continents safe and prosperous. Don't ever hesitate to give any of us a call—all of our numbers are in the email I sent."

"Thank you. For everything. I have no doubt that none of this would've happened without your help."

"I'm just glad it all worked out. That nutjob gave you quite the run for your money. Doesn't matter – you're the commander now, and it was well-deserved."

With that, the men shook hands and went their separate ways, Martin ready to settle into his new role.

3

Chapter 3

Martin sat up to his neck in electronic paperwork. The email Commander Blair had sent contained three dozen password-protected links for Martin to read and review. After the sixth document that outlined a commander's role within a war, his brain begged for a break that would never come. Little did he know the remainder of his term would follow a pattern of constant chaos, sleep coming at a premium on the rare nights he could slip away to the comforts of his own home.

Before his transformation into an office zombie, however, Martin sat behind his desk on day one of the job, spry and filled with ambition. A knock came from the door, the silhouette of a massive man filling the frosted window pane.

"Come in," Martin said, rising and crossing to the front of his desk.

The door swung open and Gerald Holmes stepped in, muscles as ripped as ever, a suitcase dragging behind him.

"Gerald, welcome!" Martin greeted, meeting his old friend for a quick hug. "How was the trip?"

"Not bad. I've gotta say, the world seems a lot more laid-back compared to the future. Crazy to remember how quickly everything turns downhill in just a couple of decades."

"Well, that's what we're here for—to stop that from happening. Is there anything I can get for you before we get started?"

"I saw the kitchen in the back—I'll go take a look myself, if you don't mind."

"No problem, I'll walk with you. Bring your bag and we can drop it in your office next door."

Martin led the way, Gerald taking a quick moment in his new office to admire the space, knowing it would soon undergo construction.

"So how did you spend election night?" Martin asked once they continued toward the kitchen.

"Quiet evening at my hotel room in Chicago—thought I'd spend some time downtown before leaving. So I got an expensive room in one of the skyscrapers. Had some dinner and drinks at the bar. Then called it a night to watch the results in bed."

"Sounds nice. The scene here was quite the opposite," Martin said with a chuckle.

Gerald faced a wall full of bins containing every snack imaginable. He decided on a packet of beef jerky and they headed back for Martin's office. "I could tell through the phone. All these young kids party hard, don't they?" He nodded to the bullpen where a majority of the staff stared at their computer screens, surely hungover.

"Yes. They definitely have more energy for those matters. I had some drinks, sure, but this place looked like a frat house a few hours after the election. I can't blame them—they worked their asses off."

Gerald grinned as they stepped into Martin's office and

closed the door behind them. He tore open the jerky and started eating like he hadn't seen food in several days.

Martin wanted nothing more than to talk with Gerald until dinner, but he had so many things to do. "So, shall we start discussing our plans? I know we're already on the same page for the most part, but we've got to iron out details."

Martin sat behind his desk and gestured for Gerald to take the open seat across the way. Gerald leaned back and placed a foot across his knee, shoulders slumping as he relaxed. "Are we even discussing anything besides killing Chris?"

Martin folded his hands together and held them in front of his lips. "We can, but I don't see the point. I think you and I are in a unique position for having been to the future—"

"I *live* there," Gerald added.

"Yes, of course. The point is, we know what's in store if we don't end this right now. Are we the last hope? I certainly hope not. But I get the sense that what we do maps out the next decade for our organization saving itself."

"I agree. Everything gradually gets worse with each passing year. Every commander after us will have to adjust more and more toward a reactive approach. Let's be proactive and just go for it."

Martin nodded. "Perfect. I want nothing more than to tear that bastard's face right off his skull. I doubt I'll get that opportunity, but why not set the bar high?"

Gerald chuckled. "You never know what will happen."

"You're the expert in these matters. What can we realistically do?" Martin leaned back, turning the floor over to his number two.

"I've been thinking a lot about this. We need to put something into motion within the next six months. I suspect he's going to keep attacking our buildings and won't stop until *we* stop him. We're past the point of beefing up security. He's going to come at us hard and frequently. I studied the diagrams we have of his mansion, and I think we can destroy it from the ground up—from the *underground*, that is."

Martin frowned, but nodded for Gerald to continue.

"We already know the cameras on his property can't reach a quarter-mile out. I'm suggesting we start drilling right outside of that range and dig a tunnel all the way to the mansion."

"No one knows what's underneath. That could end up being a massive waste of time."

"Possibly. We know there is the basement and surely parts of the mansion's foundation—that's what I want to get to. We can strap several explosives to the foundation that the house will sink into itself upon detonation. Chris won't know what happened and will be as vulnerable as he's ever been. Ideally, he'd be trapped under rubble, unable to help himself. Then we can take our time ending him."

"I like it," Martin said, sitting forward and planting his elbows on the desk. "But none of this guarantees his death. He's still invincible."

"I know that. But the objective here is to cripple him and the entire Revolution. We'd be wiping their headquarters off the map. And best case scenario, we take Chris prisoner. He may control time, but that doesn't mean he can get out of zip ties and a muzzle."

Martin chuckled at the image, both satisfying and chilling. "I'm going to have someone tail Chris. Not something we've done in a long time, but we need a clear understanding on what will kill him."

Gerald leaned forward, his chest shoulders stiff as his elbows

21

dug into his knees. "Martin, we need to discuss the obvious. I know you don't want to hear it, but we need to kill Sonya."

"Under no circumstance will I authorize that."

"But I will. I'll even do it myself if I have to. I know you have feelings for her, but you're not seeing the big picture. If she's dead, it's free game on Chris. And if we have Chris in our possession, we'd be doing the entire world a disservice by allowing Sonya to live because she tricked you into a relationship on your very first trip into the past."

Martin smacked the top of his desk with an open hand. "Don't you dare speak of that like you were there. You do not have my permission to go anywhere near Sonya."

"Look, Martin, I want to have a civil discussion about this. It's not like I'm going to look for her today. This is just a very real possibility that needs to be on your radar. And for what it's worth, my oath was sworn to the Road Runners, not to you. I will never go behind your back with a decision, but if something arises in the heat of the moment, I will do what's right for our organization. What do you think our members will do if they found out you had a chance to kill the man who caused them all so much pain, and didn't go through with it?"

Martin stared at his desk, his eyes following the random patterns of the oak.

"You wanted me here to help with the strategy and these uncomfortable decisions," Gerald continued. "That's exactly what I'm here to do. If killing one woman saves the entire continent from its pending doom, then that's a no-brainer. I'll do it every single time. Maybe your person will find something out for us and we can avoid that topic altogether. But I wanted to make sure you're clear on where I stand from day one.

"I also wish you'd see how badly she's playing you. Both her and Chris. She's living under his protection, for God's sake. Protected by the very man you're trying to kill."

"She needs protection, or else all the Road Runners who know about her connection will be after her."

"For good reason. Martin, don't you think it's possible that Chris, in all of his wisdom, has looked into his future and planted Sonya in your life from the beginning of your time travel? Or is it just a coincidence that she happened to be one of the first people you met in the past? He *knew* this moment would come, and he's using your own emotions to spare *his* life. His love for her goes as far as she's useful in keeping him alive. He won't mourn her death, because he'll be on the run looking for the next way to ensure his invincibility."

"I don't know—that all seems like a stretch. Chris is a smart man, sure, but there are a lot of gaps to fill in your theory. I just don't see him putting in all of this attention to the details."

"And I think he would. We're talking about his life and power. Who wouldn't go to ridiculous extremes to keep both?"

Martin nodded as he rubbed his temples. "I guess I can't really stop you. Just promise me that decision will only be a last resort."

"I promise I'll do whatever it takes to protect this organization."

Martin sighed. "Understood. Tell me more about this tunnel."

He got off the topic as quickly as possible. They discussed the tunnel for the next thirty minutes, but Martin's head remained distracted by how nonchalantly Gerald discussed killing Sonya. Deep down he knew it was the right decision, but that didn't mean it was one he wanted.

While they carried on their conversation, Gerald's voice

faded into background noise as Martin tried to plan for what type of candidate would need to tail Chris.

They need to be perfect.

4

Chapter 4

Chris Speidel sat in his mansion office, having just hung up the phone with Thaddeus Hamilton, the leader of the Liberation. He gazed out the window to the snow-covered landscape, forgetting how much he had taken that simple privilege for granted. With the Road Runners' office a pile of frozen rubble, he no longer had to worry of unexpected visitors to the mansion.

Needing less security at the property, he planted a couple of his guards around town, mainly keeping an eye on the airport where anyone would need to come through for reaching this remote part of the world. If the airport had no activity, the guards wandered around the small town, keeping an ear open to any chatter involving the Revolution or Road Runners.

It was always locals in town—no one actually traveled this far north unless they had specific business.

"A true time of peace?" Chris asked his empty office as he stood for a better view out the window.

Of course not. It may be peaceful in Barrow, Alaska, and even peaceful for most Revolters living around the continent, thanks to the Road Runners hiding like a bunch of frightened children. But change was coming, brewing like a vicious storm in the gray clouds where no one below could see. However, Chris was the experienced meteorologist in this shitstorm and he *did* see what was formulating.

"Martin Briar. Who would have *ever* thought?! The shy guy from Larkwood who only wanted to find out what happened to his precious little daughter." He grabbed a cup of pens and pencils from his desk and sent them crashing into the wall across the room, falling onto the couch where Commander Strike had lain days before her public execution. "GODDAMMIT!"

He didn't fear Martin directly—he feared no mere mortal—but the movement behind Martin, the blossoming of new hope like fucking azaleas in the spring, drew his concern. Even with no threats to his quiet mansion, Chris found himself with a constant sense of unease following him around like his own shadow. And it further pissed him off.

He'd taken plenty of peeks into the future to see what might come of the Road Runners' new commander, but saw nothing of noted difference. However, the future felt *different*, almost still, and foreign, despite him visiting numerous times each week. Something was off regarding the whole situation, and he refused to trust anything until Martin experienced the same fate as the commander before him.

The proper steps were already underway to ensure this, a fact that Chris needed to remind himself often as his impatience grew with each passing day. Wars didn't end overnight; multiple battles had to be won, the casualty number had to increase, all leading to a final surrender.

Tonight was the next step. His phone call with Thaddeus confirmed the evening's plans to destroy the Road Runners' office in upstate New York, not far from the old location that once housed the Council.

The Liberation had been staking out different locations to attack. With Road Runner security still depleted, they needed to strike before deciding it was time to stand up and fight—a certainty under their new leadership of Commander Briar.

Why couldn't that chickenshit have won? Chris wondered. *This whole thing would already be a done deal.*

They had to work with the results, and committed to destroying more properties to keep the Road Runners in hiding. Eventually, they'd have no more buildings to meet in and would have no choice but to stay home with the lights off and the curtains drawn.

"That's the kind of world I want to live in—a world with no Road Runners." Chris returned to his desk and opened the software—Duane's beautiful creation—that enabled him to hack into the Road Runners' television stream at will.

He clicked the necessary buttons until his computer's camera flickered to life, his face filling the screens of all Road Runner offices across the continent.

"Commander Martin Briar," he started. "I sent you a congratulatory message and have not heard back. I don't appreciate that. I know you'll see this, so *congratulations* on your historic victory into the commandership. I'm sure the Road Runners will have no regrets in choosing a man who can't even keep his own daughter alive."

He paused and let out a manic howl, leaning into the camera to capture his gaping mouth. "Now that the pleasantries are out of the way, I wanted to let all of you little Road Runners know that we are coming for you. Aggressively. Within a month, you can plan to say goodbye to many of your offices, and in turn, many of your friends.

"I'm tired. Doesn't it feel like we've been at this war for centuries? Can't it just end already? You're all ready for it, and so am I. Expect a swift end to the war within the year. We have the upper hand now and won't stop until there is nothing left to destroy. Mark my words – you'll wish you had gone with the guy who wanted to take you all to his secret island."

Chris disconnected the video on that note and started giggling. He had never seen the consequences of his video streams, but always imagined Road Runners screaming and running around their offices in a panic.

How does he keep doing this? they surely wondered. *Why can't we stop this—it should be so simple!*

Then they'd call for emergency meetings to try and dissect his message, looking for any underlying clues that might tip off, in this instance, *where* he planned on attacking next.

"You silly Road Runners will just have to wait and see!" he cackled, returning to the window to observe the world.

* * *

They agreed to no longer use suicide vests as they had done in the Barrow office—this was not some terrorist organization where people had to sacrifice themselves in order to further their agenda. Chris and Thaddeus had agreed on that much. Sure, the "Road Killers", as they liked to call themselves, understood there were still great risks for carrying out their work, but death was no longer a guarantee as a result. These were the hired hands dedicated to killing Road Runners and setting their buildings ablaze.

There had been a meeting with the Road Killers, Chris, and Thaddeus, where they all gathered to essentially watch a quarrel between the two leaders. Thaddy didn't particularly care how these bloody messes were carried out. "Use any means necessary," he had said. And Chris argued for the complete opposite, wondering why any leader with common sense would openly sacrifice members in a time where having a numbers advantage was crucial. "The Road Runners still have a massive population," Chris had explained. "Every time we lose one of our own, they gain an advantage."

Back and forth they went, the Killers watching like a tennis match. After an hour, they reached a half-hearted agreement. Bombs and arson were the preferred methods for any attacks, allowing for maximum damage to the buildings and those inside, while keeping risk to the Killers minimal.

Office size played a factor as well. Pulling off these feats in the bigger cities proved nearly impossible. Nearly.

Places like Chicago—which had multiple offices in the same city—Houston, Miami, and Denver, to name a few, were essentially off-limits thanks to the heightened security, but this left the smaller locations vulnerable to simple attacks: the upstate New York office, Sacramento, Branson, and Des Moines.

The Road Runners had no choice but to distribute their resources to their higher priority locations, but soon enough the Killers would find a way to attack even those.

Dylan Snoddy had been tasked with leading the efforts in New York, an office that housed twenty Road Runners. The Killers worked as a team, camping out a mile away from their target and preparing for a successful attack. Everyone was a specialist in their respective field. Ethan Saunders could hack the building's security system, and either cut the camera feed or replace it with a still image of the building's interior. Landon Jacobson built the actual bombs, while Frank Watts studied the building's layout and blueprint to maximize damage. All of them worked around Dylan, who served as both the unofficial leader of this pact, and also the one who had to plant the bombs around the building.

His specialty was both stealth and acting. Should he actually be caught, he knew just the right things to say to get out of a potential mess. And if they weren't buying what he was selling, no one in the group could break into a dead sprint faster than Dylan Snoddy, former college track star.

They had studied the building for the past two weeks, mainly tracking the activity of those who walked in and out, finding the best time of day to strike when the most people were inside. A two-hour window from seven to nine in the morning was the sweet spot. In their two weeks of observation they had only seen someone walk out two times, both instances to retrieve something from their cars in the parking lot.

This left Dylan practically free to roam the exterior of the building. The cameras had been frozen on still images, leaving him all the time in the world. They clearly had no concerns of being attacked in such a remote location surrounded by tall trees. Perhaps they believed the Revolution didn't know about the location – a grave mistake, for the Revolution knew everything.

Dylan enjoyed having the trees. At seven o'clock, the sun remained low in the sky, and the trees blocked most of it, leaving it to look more like dawn on the office grounds. He had planted himself behind the nearest tree, four duffel bags piled next to him that he would soon deliver to each corner of the building. He had a couple of crowbars to barricade any doors that led out of the building, a decision that typically came on the fly depending on what he saw.

"You're clear," a voice crackled from the earpiece that communicated with their main hideout a mile away, a massive tent that housed antennas, monitors, and the rest of the team.

"On my way," Dylan said, heaving the first duffel bag over his shoulder and starting his trudge toward the building. Each bag weighed thirty pounds, filled with explosives, leaving Dylan to carry one at a time to avoid being slowed down by any more weight. He had practiced his route a dozen times, learning how the bags swayed his body based on the smallest movements, like stepping over a rock, or turning the building's corner.

With an aerial map to study, Dylan calculated the exact route he'd take to avoid being seen, running back and forth from the nearest tree and planting the duffel bags strategically on each corner of the office building.

The building ran one hundred feet long by sixty feet wide – not big on paper, but seeming massive now that Dylan was running toward it with a device ready to blow it to pieces. Sweat formed around his forehead and trickled into his eyes, burning as he blinked it away. The bag no longer felt heavy over his shoulder, thanks to the hurricane of adrenaline spinning throughout his body. He briefly considered carrying more than one bag at a time, but decided sticking to the plan was the surest way to get the results needed. This was no business to make last-second changes.

Fortunately, like all other Road Runner buildings, not a single window lined the exterior, with the exception of the double glass doors that served as the entrance. His route was planned to avoid the doors, but someone could always walk out, or pull into the parking lot later than the rest of their colleagues.

Planting the bombs was the top priority, barricading the door to only be done if everything went smoothly and the situation permitted. *I can do it all,* he thought as he reached the nearest corner and dropped the bag on the ground, sliding it against the exterior's concrete surface. He brushed a quick stroke of his fingers along the wall, knowing it had been constructed to absorb a heavy blow, but having no chance to withstand what was coming. *One down, three to go.*

Dylan sprinted to the tree, slinging the second bag over his shoulder and running through the same routine, only this time to the next corner of the building. He repeated this process within two minutes, his final run taking him all the way around the building to avoid that damned entrance, and all the way back to safety at the tree that no longer hid bags, but only a couple of crowbars.

So far so good, let's do it. He grabbed one of the crowbars and dashed for the building, this time headed for the forbidden front doors. As soon as the doors entered his vision, they swung open and a man on a cell phone stepped out. At first he didn't notice Dylan charging in his direction, but after a double take and seeing the weapon, he dropped his phone on the pavement. "What the hell?!"

With a split second to make crucial decisions, Dylan looked through the glass doors, saw no one else present, and brought the crowbar over the man's head, the sound mimicking that of a baseball bat connecting crisply on a home run swing. All strength left the man's body as his head whipped to the side, blood flying from his shaggy black hair, eyes immediately rolling into his brain. He hit the ground with a dull thud, limbs splayed in every direction.

"Oh, my God!" Dylan gasped, rushing to grab the man's ankles and pull him out of sight from the doorway. He ended up dragging him toward the corner of the building he had planted the first bomb, grunting with each tug, the adrenaline helping haul the dead weight of a roughly 200-pound man.

He dashed back toward the doors where he had tossed the crowbar, picked it up, and leaped for the entrance where he slid the bar through the two door handles, pulling it snugly with the hooked end so it couldn't fall off with the inevitable banging on the doors that would soon begin.

Run.

The coast remained clear from that front entrance, but he still sprinted away like his life depended on it. "Everything's planted," he shouted for his earpiece to transmit. "Blow it up!"

"Copy that," the crackling voice replied.

Dylan skidded to a stop, his shoes sinking into the earth that had been just moist enough to leave a muddy ring around his soles. The bombs were connected through a radio device controlled back at the tent. One push of a button would simultaneously detonate them, collapsing the four corners of the building and entrapping everyone while a fire would quietly engulf them all.

He had run at least 1,000 feet away from the building, looking at the office through the trees, staying behind one in case any flying shrapnel soared his direction.

"All clear," the earpiece said, and within five seconds Dylan heard the rumbling boom, the ground vibrating as the bombs exploded.

5

Chapter 5

The next morning, Martin personally reached out to the other commanders and asked for their help in rounding up the best and brightest minds. It was time to really study his ability as a Warm Soul.

"If we can find a way to replicate my Warm Soul and implant it in others, we can end this war tomorrow." He had said this on a conference call with the commanders, Gerald sitting across the desk as he listened with a balled fist under his chin.

"Commander Briar," Commander Quang said, "We appreciate what you're trying to do, but you have bigger issues at hand. This is detracting from your time to respond to the attacks from yesterday. Your focus is in the wrong area."

"With all due respect, Commander," Martin replied. "I disagree. We've exhausted the tried and true methods of responding to these attacks. Yet here we are with another. And there will surely be more. My goal is to remove Chris from power and put the Revolution in a position with no leader. As it stands, we have no ways of getting to him. I'm not going to sit here and authorize the same old things we've done in the past that never achieve results. We need to try something different, and if I have to sacrifice my body and time to do so, I'm game."

"I appreciate your lofty goals," Commander Quang replied. "But we have gone through these tests with Commander Blair. Nothing has ever been found. Warm Souls are the great and elusive mystery of our time-travel universe."

"That's no excuse to not keep trying. It's either this, or I put myself in the line of danger by using my ability to get to Chris. Would you like to have *another* special election to replace a dead commander?"

"May I?" Commander Blair chimed in before Quang replied again. "Look, Martin, you don't need any sort of approval to do this. We're just suggesting it's a waste of your time. It's unlikely that anything new will come to fruition after more studies. The team who studied you initially has tons of files on their research, and they all point back to nothing. Again, do as you see fit, but it may be better to focus your efforts into a different game plan."

Martin crossed his arms and frowned. This was a conference call without video, so he didn't need to worry about his appearance. Gerald smirked as Martin started shaking his head. "You know this could be over already if you just sent some help. What would Chris do if 50,000 Road Runners showed up at his front door?"

"It's not that simple, and you know it," Quang fired back. "Aside from our Bylaws, gathering that many of us in one location would surely expose us to the general public, especially in that small Alaskan town."

"You know that this affects all of us. All around the world. His counterparts may not be as evil or aggressive on your continents, but what makes you think he will stop with North

America? He will keep taking everything he can get until he's stopped. Commander Iglesia, Chris will surely start with South America once he has control of the North. Are you ready to fight what would be a massive army of his by then?"

"We have a strong relationship with the leader of the Re-volters down here," Commander Iglesia said. "They've assured us protection from anything related to Chris Speidel. Sorry, Commander Briar."

Martin sighed under his breath, sure to turn his head away from the speaker phone. "You guys don't understand. You don't know him like I do. He is manipulative, a professional con man who will do anything for power. You may have a good relationship with them for now, but what happens when Chris offers them the world? They're already on the same team—it won't take much."

"Again, Commander, it's just not a concern for us."

Martin wanted to punch a hole through his desk. "The greatest mistake a society can make is to follow the belief of 'it will never happen here.' We've seen it over and over throughout history. Genocide, famine, drought, and disease have all plagued different countries at one point in time. All could have been avoided, but we buckle into our beliefs that such tragedies will never befall us. I have news for you: it will happen. Don't let your arrogance get in the way, and please try to understand how dangerous and devious this man is."

The line was silent, the only sound someone sniffling in the background. "That's a good thought and all," Commander Iglesia finally replied. "But we're not going to do anything until he becomes a direct threat to our countries."

"I think we've beat this dead horse enough," Commander Blair said. "Martin, no one is sending reinforcements. If you want to run tests on yourself, then go for it, just don't count on us for any support. Does anyone have anything else they'd like to discuss on this call?"

Commander Blair had just silenced Martin, and the thought made him fume. They all tersely wished each other farewell, Martin sitting quietly as the call disconnected.

"We're on our own," he said to Gerald.

"It appears so. What do you want to do?"

"Do you think it's a waste of time?"

"I think we can start with a blood sample. Let our people study it in a lab and see if they come up with anything. Beyond that, I'm not sure what you'd like to do. It's not like you can even freeze time—you need someone else for that."

Martin rubbed his forehead. Sleep had been impossible to come by, the stress of getting this organization back on its feet weighing down on him every second of the day. That wasn't even considering that they still had no surefire way of capturing Chris. Gerald had already gathered a team to start constructing the underground tunnel in Alaska, but they were still a week out from breaking ground, and likely another two weeks from then to complete the project.

"Am I in over my head, Gerald? Be honest with me."

"No," he replied quickly. "You're ambitious—something we desperately need right now. I think you're just spreading yourself too thin. You need to reel in your focus. Let me work on the tunnel – that's going to be our way of getting Chris, I'm sure of it. And your only worry should be rebuilding our infrastructure and gaining the public's trust."

Martin shrugged. "I guess. I just know these two years are going to fly so fast. We literally have to take huge strides every single day if we want any sort of legacy to look back on."

"And we are. You just don't feel it. You haven't been out in public yet. People are hopeful again—even the people who voted to hide. You've already inspired the confidence in our group that had vanished when he kidnapped Commander Strike. Just keep pressing a little bit each day, and I promise, in the end, you're gonna look back and not believe what you achieved."

Martin nodded his head slowly, feeling motivated himself. "Thanks, Gerald. I needed that. You wanted to discuss the tunnel today?"

"Yes," he said, sitting forward. "I've been running numbers. If we hire on eight more people to help with the tunnel, we can shave another week off the construction. We'd also get to start sooner, as in the next three days or so."

"Are there people willing to work?"

There had been a shortage of Road Runners willing to contribute, mainly due to the fear keeping them locked in their homes.

"We have lines of people willing to get on this project. Like I said, you've inspired the masses. They want in. They're fed up with living in fear and realize that Chris is the reason for it. This project is going to go very smoothly, based on the initial response I've received."

"Then hire whoever you need. Let's move on this." The additional spending request had to go through Martin's approval. With a little under one trillion dollars in the Road Runners' bank account, he saw no reason to decline any expenses that involved capturing Chris. Besides, they still had teams traveling into the past to buy stocks that would explode over time. The cash flow remained constant as long as they were placing sound investments.

"Thank you. Have you had a chance to look through the list of potential Council members?"

Martin had delegated some of the tasks in his initial email from Commander Blair. Some of the matters required both of their attention, mainly the one where they needed to rebuild a Council to govern the organization. "I looked through some of them, and I just don't know. Did you get the feeling that you kept reading the same profile over and over? It's like all of these candidates are the same person."

Gerald chuckled. "They are all highly educated people with ample judicial or government experience. So yes, most of them have similar backgrounds and job histories. They're all very much qualified."

Martin nodded. "I do want *some* experience on the Council, but I also want some fresh blood. I'm going to look heavily into candidates with strong education, but *no* government experience. We need some free thinkers on the Council who will challenge the norm. These are desperate times and we can't fall back on our same old habits. Have you made any outreach calls?"

One of Martin's first assignments was to contact all existing Council members and see if they planned on returning to their jobs. He had personally placed phone calls, while a team of Road Runners went on a search for their Councilors. Their homes had all been abandoned, and it was clear they remained in hiding.

"I've made a couple of calls, but no luck," Gerald said. "I don't think any of them are coming back, Boss."

"I think they need to hear the right message. I was hoping it wouldn't come to this, but I'm going to broadcast a speech directed to the Council. If we can't find them, then we just need to call them out of hiding. Surely they're somewhere watching."

"Why don't they have tracking devices like the rest of the leadership team?"

Martin shrugged. "Because they didn't want them. And they make the laws. No one can tell them otherwise."

"Should we find candidates who would be open to that?"

"Why would anyone be *open* to having a tracking device implanted? What we need to worry about is making sure something like this never happens again. No reason for our leaders to disappear because their lives are threatened. Honestly, I don't like the tracking." Martin tapped on his inner bicep where his had been implanted. "Maybe we should find a Council who wants to get rid of them. No need for us to invade anyone's privacy."

"I'm sure that will be a hearty discussion, but we need to focus on the bigger picture. This is the Council, and you get to shape it. The people you choose are your legacy and will remain in their positions well after you're gone. You can single-handedly shape the future of this organization."

Martin understood this just fine and had already wrestled with the overwhelming responsibility. One bad decision could hamper their growth for years. He had many factors to consider like a candidate's beliefs, age, and history on particular issues. The new Council would be a direct reflection of his tenure as commander, no one in the past ever having the opportunity to fill more than two seats during their term. He had seven to fill, assuming none of the prior members returned.

"Okay, let's come up with a list of finalists."

6

Chapter 6

They discussed potential Council replacements for an hour, but the conversation veered in another direction, as it tended to in the midst of brainstorming. Martin brought up the idea of having someone travel back in time and tail Chris to truly learn something that could be useful in this war against him.

Gerald hadn't liked the idea at first, deeming it an unnecessary risk, but eventually saw its value. This wasn't a matter of having someone infiltrate Chris's life, but rather observe from a safe distance. It would be planned with the Road Runner's safety as the top priority, information on Chris a close second.

Once they agreed on a general plan for the mission, they shifted their focus to potential recruits. It was a delicate matter, one that wouldn't move forward without the perfect person to fill the role.

Their dream candidate needed mental strength off the charts, expert espionage abilities, no fear of death. A bad ass.

Gerald knew plenty of people who fit this mold from his vigilante work in the grim future, so they punched in name after name into the computer, reading over profiles and narrowing the selection down to three finalists.

Martin projected his computer screen to the 80-inch monitor hanging on the wall in the conference room. His office had one more week of construction. Gerald's was expected to be completed in three days—his requiring less upgrades. Until then, they bounced around the various conference rooms.

"How quickly are you wanting to move on this?" Gerald asked, rubbing his tired eyes. It was eight o'clock, just about time for bed after working since seven in the morning.

"Immediately. Any chance we can get these three in here tomorrow for interviews?"

Gerald nodded. "We should, assuming they're not already in the middle of other missions."

"Perfect. Let's reach out to them and see what we can arrange, then call it a night. I'd love to get this project started the day after tomorrow if we can swing it."

Gerald whipped out his cell phone to make the calls.

* * *

They managed some sleep, a quick six hours that was nowhere near enough for what lay ahead. The growing exhaustion reminded Martin of the time when Izzy was a baby, every day seeming worse than the one before, his brain begging for a rest but knowing deep down it was never coming. Eventually he found a way to power through it all, even turn his fatigue into energy, if such a thing was possible.

That had been in his twenties, and he doubted his middle-aged body could handle such abuse now. He had no choice but to find out.

Gerald had phoned the three potential candidates for the dangerous role of tailing Chris, but only one was available to come in. As Martin feared, the other two were already in the middle of other missions to which they had been assigned.

Fortunately, the candidate who was on her way to the office was also Gerald's favorite of the lot. And if she made a splash in this initial interview, there would be no need to question the others.

Gerald joined Martin in a conference room as they awaited their interviewee's arrival.

"She's the real deal," he said. "I worked with her on a mission in the late 2020's, right before things got completely out of control. You've seen her resume; there's not a single weakness on there."

"I agree. Read it this morning, and I'm very intrigued."

A knock came from the door and Martin rose to answer it.

"Sir," one of his staff members greeted. "Your ten o'clock is here."

The man stepped aside and gave way to a beautiful woman with smooth, olive skin, round brown eyes, and flowing honey-brown hair.

"Commander Briar?" she asked, sticking out a hand.

Martin grabbed her hand, feeling a world of strength in her grip. "You must be Arielle Lucila. It's a pleasure to meet you."

"The pleasure's all mine, sir," she replied, and her eyes bulged when she saw Gerald sitting in the room behind Martin. "Oh my God!" she squealed like a teenager. "I didn't know you would be in this interview, too."

Martin stepped aside to let her pass, and she brushed by with her arms held out as Gerald stood up.

43

Arielle slapped him on his beefy arms. "Why didn't you say so on the phone last night?"

Gerald grinned. "I thought I'd surprise you."

They hugged for a moment before Arielle stepped back in search of a chair to sit. She was surprisingly short, perhaps no more than five-and-a-half feet tall. Martin had met plenty of these type of specialists, and whether a man or woman, they were always built like different-sized versions of Gerald.

Arielle wore a gray blazer that matched her skirt. In all the commotion, Martin didn't notice the clacking of her heels until she had crossed the table to sit down across from Gerald. Her calf muscles bulged, and Martin knew the rest of her was likely just as solid.

Martin closed the door and returned to his spot next to Gerald. "Arielle, thank you so much for flying out here on such short notice. Have you been to Colorado before?"

"Been here? I was born and raised here. I grew up in Aurora, and didn't leave until I went to college in Chicago. Loved it there so much I decided to stay."

"Ahhh, very nice. I'm also a native—from Larkwood."

"I know Larkwood, had a few cousins who lived out there, although I don't think they are still there. Who knows? I travel around so much I hardly remember what year I'm in."

Arielle giggled as if this amused her. As absurd of a lifestyle as it seemed, Martin had to remind himself that some people enjoyed it, even thrived in the constant chaos.

"So *when* are you originally from?" Martin asked. She didn't look any older than thirty, but that didn't mean anything in this life of time travel.

"This is my real time in 2020. I was born in 1994."

"You're only *twenty-six*?" Martin gasped, and he saw Gerald smirk out of the corner of his eye.

Arielle shrugged. "On paper, I suppose. But if you add up all of my work for the Road Runners, I have nearly two hundred years of experience."

Martin tossed his hands in the air. "I'm impressed. Can you tell me about some of your experience? Your resume lists 'classified missions'. Would you mind going into detail about those?"

"As much as I can. I've done lots of highly sensitive work for Commander Strike, and Commander Porter before her."

Martin moved forward in his seat and nodded for her to continue.

"I can't go into specific results of my missions, but I can let you know what I was doing. My first major one was the JFK assassination. I stalked several persons of interest, including Kennedy, to see what I could learn."

"How did you stalk the president?" Martin asked. "I can't imagine you were able to sneak into the White House."

"I joined the Secret Service. Traveled back a few years with a resume formulated to get the job. I took all of the courses the Road Runners used to offer: espionage, deception, Ninjutsu to name a few. I don't know why we stopped offering those. I suppose because we don't do much mission work aside from trying to stop the future from happening."

Martin looked to Gerald for clarity, still too new to the organization to know its history.

"We used to have teams go on missions to learn history," Gerald explained. "Find truths, and sometimes stop tragic events from happening. They were called the Angel Runners."

"We are *still* called that," Arielle added. "Don't count us as extinct. We still exist, just not as many as there used to be."

45

"Interesting," Martin said.   "I'll have to look more into that—sounds fascinating.   Back to our topic though. Kennedy—who did it?"

"Not a detail I can give. Let's just say it's complicated, and we really had no way of stopping it."

"Of course. What other work have you done?"

"Pretty much any high-profile matters you can think of within the United States. I also looked at Lincoln's assassination. MLK's. Tried to stop the Great Depression, the Vietnam War, and 9/11. I studied the Revolutionary War up close to see what we might be able to apply in the future. Those just scratch the surface. I'm pretty much *always* on a mission. Tomorrow I'm supposed to head to another, trying to stop some murder in Florida."

"If I may," Martin said, leaning forward even more, "I think we may be cancelling that mission. What are your thoughts on this potential one with Chris?"

Arielle's eyes lit up, and her hands clenched the chair's arm. "What all does it entail? Gerald only told me that it would be following Chris. But I'm sure there's more to it than that."

"Would you like to elaborate, Gerald?" Martin asked.

"Certainly," Gerald said, crossing his arms. "We're looking for information. Chris is immortal—as we all know—but there *has* to be a way for him to die, or to even reverse his invincibility. We've tried infiltrating his inner circle in the past, but he always sniffs it out. We're just about done with that option, and instead want someone to follow him and blend into the background. Sure, you may not get the inside scoop being in every room as him, but you may be able to learn something. I know you have the technology: hidden cameras, bugs, and all that. This mission is completely one to proceed at your own risk—as you see fit. We're not going to demand you do anything besides report back with your daily findings. How far you push the envelope is completely up to you."

"I understand. I'm not afraid to take chances, but won't make dumb mistakes either. How long of a mission is this?"

"As long as it takes," Gerald replied calmly. "No timeline. We'd expect you to go back to the time before Chris was even involved in the time travel world. Study what changed him. He surely wasn't always this demon—or maybe he was. But we've got to know everything about him."

"We can compensate you," Martin said while Arielle looked at the ceiling. "You name the price."

She scrunched her face. "Fifteen million sound good?"

"Done." Martin stood and stretched his hand over the desk for Arielle to shake. "Welcome to the team. You'll be reporting directly to Gerald. Are you good to start tomorrow?"

"Absolutely I am." She had a wide grin, and turned her attention to Gerald. "I guess they just couldn't keep us apart. Glad to be working with you again."

"You're gonna do big things for us," Gerald said. "I just know it."

"Shall we have a drink in my office to celebrate?" Martin asked. "Assuming the construction crew hasn't cleaned out my drawers."

They shared a laugh as they exited the conference room and started down the hallway, Martin beaming with pride at his first major accomplishment as commander.

7

Chapter 7

"Today will change the future for all of us," Thaddeus said to his room full of Road Killers, a fairly mixed group of Revolters and Liberators. "Las Vegas had long been a hideout for the Road Runners—an easy place to hide. It's even easier when you own a hotel and casino behind the Strip. Now, I wonder that would happen if the whole building came crashing down?"

The people in the room howled like loons, some of them whistling and clapping at the violent threats, prompting Thaddeus to raise his arms to hush the crowd.

"Simmer down. There's plenty for everyone to do. As you've read in your reports, it's going to be a complete takeover before we blow it to the sky. Like the desert needs any more heat, am I right?"

They broke into excited laughter.

"Timing is the most important thing today. The hotel has thirty-six floors, and we'll be starting the fires on the penthouse at *exactly* two o'clock. Every floor has someone assigned to it to start their own fires, but you must stick to the schedule to ensure the person on the floor above you has had time to escape. Remember to avoid elevators, as they are likely to be halted during an emergency. If we stick to the plan, we'll create a domino effect with the fire, and the entire building will be up in flames by 3:12 sharp. You will see your colleagues running in the stairwell with you. That's why I asked you all to specifically wear solid black hats today. If you see someone *not* in a black hat while you're escaping, shoot them. Watch out for bodies when you're descending the stairs. Thirty-six floors is a lot to cover—there's bound to be hotel guests making a run for it. Are we clear?"

All seventy people in the room nodded silently.

"Perfect. Remember to stick to your role. If you're assigned to setting a floor on fire and run into any issues, abandon your floor at the scheduled time. There will be more than enough to make up for it."

Thaddeus paused to check his watch.

"It's 11:30 now. Take the next hour to relax, maybe grab a drink. Then grab your bottle of kerosene and let's head over at 12:30 to get into our positions. And most importantly, don't forget to have fun!"

This received a final round of hollering from the rowdy group. They had rented a meeting space in the Rio Hotel and Casino, just across the street from the Road Runner-owned Desert Oasis, an off-Strip casino and hotel meant to rival Rio and The Palms. Before the sun would set for the night, the Desert Oasis would no longer exist.

The Road Runners held many of their secret meetings in the hotel's underground, often containing upward of 400 members at any given time.

400, Thaddeus kept thinking, smirking every time the number popped into his head. If that wouldn't put a damper on the

Road Runners' collective spirits, then nothing would. By far the biggest massacre in their bloody history, Thaddeus was just glad to be the one leading the charge.

It had been a grueling six months finding the right talent to pull off such an enormous task. Once the team was built, they needed to quickly infiltrate the proper businesses within the city, mainly the Desert Oasis hotel. Forty members of the team were hotel staff, hired on months ago in various roles to learn the ins and outs. They picked a day far out enough to guarantee they each had the day off to avoid any suspicion from the hotel management. Out of a total staff of 8,000, no one had the time to realize the connection between those who had requested the time off.

Because the Road Runners messed up, Thaddeus thought. It wasn't necessarily the Road Runners' fault—they didn't have the numbers to staff an entire hotel of their own. But they didn't even bother installing a single member who dealt with the day-to-day, keeping themselves to positions of upper management who never mingled with hotel guests. Perhaps if they had sprinkled a few of their own among the front desk staff, the cleaning crew, and even the restaurant, they might have noticed the group of Revolters and Liberators infiltrating.

But none of that happened, and they were now hours away from ending the existence of the newest attraction in Las Vegas. No more gourmet buffet, no more rooftop night clubs and swimming pools. Just a massive pile of forgotten memories.

The anticipation pulsed under his skin, so Thaddeus decided to leave the Rio and get a head start. He had the entire team connected on the same radio channel, and his role was to stand on the outside corner to keep an eye on any potential police or firefighter activity that might arrive too early.

When he stepped outside of the Rio, the typical wave of heat suffocated him, but he hardly noticed as he kept his gaze focused on the massive building across the street. The Desert Oasis had an exterior of golden windows, meant to look like sand in the desert, but just a shade darker. The building stood in the slightest U-curve, centering around the roundabout that served as the main entrance where limousines, taxis, and pedestrians alike packed into the area. The sun currently beat down on the back side of the hotel, leaving the front in a dark shade and sparing the eyes of anyone looking at its usual blinding glare.

"You are a magnificent building," he said. "It's really a shame to tear all of this down for 400 Road Runners, but I suppose it's the message we're sending as well."

They had all grown an appreciation for the hotel, seeing as many of them spent the past six months working there. But like any dirty business, it was best to keep personal feelings out of the mix. He crossed the street and waited in the blistering heat for the next thirty minutes as the team gradually arrived.

* * *

The events started promptly at two o'clock. Moments before, everyone had given a quick shout into their radios to confirm that all were functioning. Thaddeus kept his volume low, and the radio held to his ear like a cell phone to keep any wandering eyes from spotting him looking suspicious. It was nearly impossible to stand out in Las Vegas, considering how many people flooded the sidewalks at any given moment, but he couldn't take any chances. Not this time. Today was about executing a carefully planned drill.

"Fire is set on the penthouse, beginning my descent," the first voice crackled through the radio.

Thaddeus gazed to the massive structure, knowing all hell was about to break loose inside.

"Fire is set on the 35th floor, beginning my descent," the next voice announced.

They were each given instruction to inform of their progress in this specific manner, a virtual countdown for Thaddeus watching outside. From their calculations, a fire wouldn't likely be visible until they had set floors 19 through 36 ablaze—flames and smoke possibly showing from the rooftop. Even with a gallon of kerosene per floor, fires needed time to grow and eventually rage beyond control.

It took exactly ten seconds to run down one flight of stairs, rounding a corner with each. They calculated no more than ten minutes for the person on the penthouse to reach the safety of ground level, and that factored in plenty of time for progressing fatigue.

A voice crackled through the radio every two minutes as planned. No issues or mistakes through the first half hour, for the first fifteen floors. Slightly ahead of schedule, however, was the sight of black smoke oozing from the top of the hotel. It wasn't much, likely overlooked by the thousands of people below, but Thaddeus knew what it was, and grinned at the sight.

"We have smoke, people," he said into his radio, covering his mouth to keep his words for their intended audience. "Nothing to worry about yet, no one out here is paying any attention. Keep up the good work and stay on schedule."

The 18th floor announced their fire had been set, and they were now halfway finished. It would be another half hour until all members would be safely out of the building, but flames would certainly start to grow within the next few minutes.

Thaddeus paced back and forth, making an effort to not hold his gaze on the building. People walked by and paid him no attention, many of them entering the hotel as if the whole thing weren't about to come crashing down.

He gasped at the first sight of a flame, the fiery orange breaking through the glass of the second floor from the top. "Holy shit!" Thaddeus exclaimed, a slight laugh escaping his lips. Still no one seemed to notice, so he practically whispered into his radio, "We have flames. Visible flames from the 35th floor."

Just as he said that, more windows blew out with monstrous clouds of fire, black smoke immediately following, chunks of glass clearly raining from above.

"What the fuck?!" someone nearby shouted. Thaddeus swiveled around to see a young man likely in Vegas for the first time as a legal adult, eyes drawn to the top of the hotel. A crowd gathered behind him and followed his stare to the tragic scene.

"Did something crash into the hotel?" a horrified woman asked, shielding her eyes as she gawked upward.

"I didn't see anything," another said.

"Where are we?" Thaddeus whispered into the radio and moving it straight to his ear. The radio had sounded during the commotion, but he could hardly hear over the excitement brewing outside.

"Floor fourteen, sir," someone replied.

"Let's keep it moving. Should be plenty of time, no need to

53

panic yet."

Sirens had yet to sound in the distance, a good sign. And even once they did, it would take time for the emergency vehicles to reach the hotel. In all, they likely had ten more minutes before anyone arrived, and even then, their focus would be on the upper floors, not the fires burning everywhere else.

In a matter of minutes, the crowd gathering on the corner intersection had swelled to at least one hundred people, many wandering over from the busy Strip. They watched helplessly as smoke and flames poured from the building, the chatter rising to a near panic.

"Has any one called 9-1-1 yet?" a woman asked.

"I did!" three different people shouted back.

Sirens whined in the distance, prompting all of the by-standers to look around. Thaddeus knew the nearest fire station was one mile away—they might have even been able to see the flames as they loaded into the truck. Traffic had halted on the main road, everyone stopping to watch what would happen next, sure to cause a jam for the approaching firetruck.

More glass blew out, bringing everyone's attention back to the building.

"No!" someone screamed. "Don't do it!"

Thaddeus didn't understand, but looked up in time to see the small blip of a figure jump out of the shattered window, limbs twirling in the air like an acrobat. Time seemed to have slowed to a snail's pace during that fall, but in reality it only took five seconds for that poor soul to splatter on the ground, exploding like a bug on a windshield.

"Ohmygod," an older man mumbled, clutching his stomach as he forced his way through the crowd to vomit in the same grass where Thaddeus stood.

The group fell eerily silent, the only sounds that of the screeching fire sirens, now a couple blocks away, and the crackling of the fire that had grown to engulf the upper six floors.

It appeared that no one inside realized what was occurring—only a handful of people had run out.

Thaddeus raised his radio and whispered, "Send in the barricades."

Like everything else that had been planned to the finest detail, Thaddeus wanted minimal numbers exiting through the main entrance. Two double-decker buses had parked along the long driveway that led to the entrance's roundabout, right where they were supposed to be. These drivers were part of the team, having driven these buses for the last three months up and down the Strip.

Their job was to crash the buses into the main entrance and impede the doors. Their engines roared, loud enough to be heard over the sirens that were now navigating through a sea of cars, having less luck than Moses trying to part the Red Sea. The tires squealed, sending small puffs of smoke onto the sidewalk where a dozen people jumped away in fright.

They peeled off, swerving at first, one bus following the other like marching ants, but regaining control just in time. All eyes focused on the buses, the flames above a mere afterthought in the heat of the moment. The lead bus barreled through a limousine and two taxi cabs, metal crunching like 1,000 cans of soda in unison. The few people who remained at the hotel entrance realized the bus was coming in their direction and scattered like flies being shooed. They gasped and screamed, everyone dodging the over-sized vehicles.

The path had been cleared and both buses rammed into the building, causing the glass doors to shatter, their remnants spread all over the ground like snow. The bus doors swung open on both vehicles, each with a tumbling man leaping from the short stairs and dashing away from the hotel without looking back.

Just as they had done so, the first firetruck arrived, following the same path as the buses, but stopping short of the entrance where nine firefighters jumped out and immediately looked to the top of the hotel. A couple darted toward the smashed entrance, while three more started unraveling the hose.

They think the fire's only up there, Thaddeus thought with a grin. *They don't even know the worst is yet to come.*

He had his radio near his head and listened as his team stuck to the plan inside. They were down to the fifth floor, ten more minutes before everything would be set aflame. They could probably all make a run for it and still be fine, but Thaddeus wasn't one to cut corners. They had a plan that was working brilliantly, no point in stopping it now.

A second firetruck arrived, swerving down the sidewalk as their colleagues surely had informed them of the erupting chaos. More firefighters scrambled from the truck, bolting for the two buses and rocking them back and forth in a desperate attempt to move them.

They didn't budge and Thaddeus chuckled to himself, knowing they had specifically picked those vehicles for that reason.

"Are we clear yet?" he asked into the radio.

"Last floor," a panicked voice cried in response.

"Perfect, let's get the dynamite ready, folks. We have the scene we need out here."

Thaddeus pushed his way through the crowd that had easily

grown to 500 ogling people. The building would implode and collapse within itself, very much a controlled demolition, but he wanted to be further away just in case any debris managed to fly outward.

"We're all clear, sir," the radio said.

"In two minutes, detonate the bombs," Thaddeus said calmly, like it was an order he had given hundreds of times in his life.

Everyone from inside had been instructed to run south from the building, the opposite direction of the growing crowd where Thaddeus blended in. Two minutes was plenty of time for someone in a dead sprint to get away before it all came crashing down.

Thaddeus took one last chance to savor the moment, admiring what he managed to put together. Surely Chris would approve, but he didn't really care what the old man thought. This turned into a much more gorgeous gathering than he had anticipated, and this whole crowd had a front row seat to watch the collapse—both literally and figuratively—of the Road Runners.

With a smirk unraveling across his face, Thaddeus checked his watch and spoke into the radio. "It's showtime, folks. Thank you for all of your hard work today. Bring this beautiful building down."

He powered off the radio and tossed it in a nearby trashcan, walking away from the booming sound of explosions and screams.

8

Chapter 8

The Road Runners had long held an open-door policy. All members were welcome to visit any offices, and even request meetings with local leadership, all the way up to the commander.

They had always been a peaceful bunch, too, until the televised execution of Commander Strike. Now, members lived on edge and would rather give up their unique lives as Road Runners instead of living in fear from Chris Speidel and his supporters.

Martin had insisted on keeping his headquarters in the downtown Denver office, and at the time there hadn't been any reason to doubt the decision. Road Runners had fallen completely inactive and uninvolved with the day-to-day operations of their organization, and the office was a shell of what it once had been.

Martin's election, however, brought out a fresh wave of confidence for many, even those who remained furious with the organization for failing to complete any rescue mission for Strike. A split had divided the organization, members taking polarized stances on how to best handle that delicate situation of either sacrificing Martin Briar, a nobody at the time, or letting Chris carry out his twisted game with Strike.

"You need to address these people," Gerald said.

They sat in Martin's finished office, now equipped with everything from a kitchen and pantry, to a wall of monitors for varied purposes. The furniture had all been swapped out, too, replaced with a new oak desk, two couches, and a glass coffee table in the massive space. They had knocked down walls to two adjoining rooms to make way for the commander's office, essentially converting it into a second home.

His favorite feature—at least for today—was the sound-proofed walls. He didn't understand how any of it worked, but once his door closed the office became engulfed in pure, glorious silence.

Currently, on the other side of his door were about fifty Road Runners, at least thirty of them members who did not work in Denver. The entire organization had watched in shock as news broadcasts from around the country showed a Las Vegas hotel oozing flames and debris before eventually collapsing into itself. They spared none of the gore or disturbing imagery of frightened people jumping from shattered windows.

The country mourned the loss of so many innocent lives—close to 4,000 based on early reporting, and certain to climb. But the Road Runners absorbed another devastating blow, losing 400 of their members who either worked or lived within the hotel, their biggest official structure in the world.

Martin hadn't known its role in the Road Runners until he went on the campaign trail. He had given a speech in one of the hotel's smaller ballrooms, jam-packed with every Road Runner who lived in the area. They had been a warm audience, happy to host him and showering him with hospitality. They had even offered him and the campaign team the presidential suite for the night, but they had to decline to move on to the next city.

Good lives were lost, and he was sorry that he hadn't known them better. The members, however, didn't want an apology. They wanted action. Immediately.

The Road Runners who had barged into the Denver office, demanding a word with Commander Briar, all had connections to the Las Vegas hotel. Some had lost friends and family. Others were simply shaken up that the Revolters were capable of such terrorism. The hope Martin had originally sparked now mixed with outrage, and the result was a fed up membership directing their disgust toward their new leader.

It had first started with a group of three women wandering into the office, informing Martin that they each had husbands on official Road Runner business in the hotel. With no survivors reported, they came demanding a statement from Martin, urging him to commit to a plan of retaliation.

Martin consoled the women, offering his deepest sympathy, and assuring them he was already hard at work with Gerald in finding a way to bring Chris to justice. They had nodded quietly and sat in silence for a few more seconds before one of the women started shouting at Martin, crying that he should have been sacrificed for Commander Strike.

Gerald had to escort the women out of Martin's office, but let them remain in the building, Martin willing to converse as long as it remained civil. Little did he know how distant civility was at the moment for the entire organization, never mind these particular three individuals. Within an hour, more people had arrived, and Martin didn't know if the women had called them

60

in for backup, or if they showed up on their own. But they all demanded a word with their new commander.

Those who worked in the office were trying to continue their daily tasks, but the distractions became too much when the crowd of angry members started chants of "Remove Briar!" and "Recall the vote!"

The rage grew palpable within the office, but no one was violent, one thing they had all been grateful for. Gerald volunteered to calm down the scene, believing his mere presence would intimidate the riled up membership. While he managed to stop the chants, these particular members buckled in for the long haul, making themselves at home in the kitchen and lounge area, conversing with each other, and not afraid if their heated discussions were overheard by the rest of the office.

"Can we set up a stream to show in just this building?" Martin asked Gerald. "I don't exactly want to let these people into my office—who knows how they'll act once face-to-face with me?"

Gerald nodded. "I don't see why not. Don't you think it's a good idea to address the entire organization, though? If not, I imagine more people will be showing up to speak with you."

Martin leaned back in his chair and rubbed his eyes. "Yes, you're probably right. Can you bring in one of the people who were chanting for a recall vote?"

"Yes, sir."

Gerald left the office. If these people would listen, they'd understand that Martin and Gerald were taking this seriously and working on a plan. This wasn't a matter of attacking Chris on a whim—that method had been tried over and over to no avail. Chris was always prepared, never caught off guard.

Gerald returned with a man who appeared to be in his thirties, with spiky blond hair and a pair of sunglasses over his reddened face, clearly back from a recent vacation in the sun. Martin had looked the same way while living in the Caribbean.

"Good afternoon," Martin greeted, standing to shake the man's hand before sitting back down. "What is your name, sir?"

"Troy Percival," he replied flatly.

Martin felt Troy's eyes burning through those sunglasses, scanning him like a calculating hawk. "What brings you into the office today?"

Troy crossed his arms as his brows furrowed. "Are you serious? You don't know why any of us are in the office?"

"Of course I do. I asked what brought *you* in specifically. Did you have a relative in Vegas?"

Troy shook his head. "No, fortunately I didn't lose anyone in the attacks. I'm just a Road Runner who has had enough of the incompetent leadership. I didn't like Strike, but I *really* didn't like how we just let her die . . . for you." Troy looked Martin up and down like he was shit on the sidewalk. "Everything used to feel so secure. Even when we knew the dangers of Chris, life never felt threatened. But ever since the scandal with Strike and her team killing each other, things have just spiraled out of control."

"I get it," Martin interjected. "Everything is uncertain right now. We're working on it. But I need to know why and how many people are already discussing a recall vote. I've hardly had time to learn the ropes. Hell, this office was just finished two days ago—I've been working out of conference rooms."

Troy nodded. "Look, Commander, I'm sure you're a good man with good intentions. Believe it or not, none of this is personal despite the hateful comments you're hearing. For many of us, the election was too close. Half of our organization voted for Templeton—we really do want to disappear and pretend none of this ever happened. We begged for a recount, but were assured the technology made no errors. We accepted that, but still strongly believe you're the absolutely wrong person for the job. In times like this, we need a familiar face, someone with a lifetime of experience dealing with Chris and this sort of conflict. Someone intimidating and threatening. No one has a reason to trust you, and between the Strike debacle and the tight election, conspiracy theories are starting to swirl. And now people are dying in multiple attacks all over the country. Road Runners are scared to step foot outside, and we have no backbone to turn to."

Martin raised a hand for Troy to stop. "I really appreciate you having this conversation with me in such a civil manner—this has not been the approach others have taken so far. Let me level with you, Troy. I have no idea why they wanted me to run for this position. I promise you that I was just as confused every step of the way. It didn't make sense when they first asked, or when I started trending upward in early polling, or even on the night I won. I'd be lying if I told you I completely know what I'm doing.

"But I will tell you that Chris murdered my mother. And not in the way where he plays mind games. No, he broke into my home and slaughtered my mother. I am hell-bent on killing him. That alone may not qualify me for this job, but you can rest assured my goals are bringing justice to Chris and peace for the rest of us. I've surrounded myself with the best talent. Gerald here is one of the smartest and most fearless people I know. He's also a brilliant strategist—he helped me get in and out of the future unharmed. We're working around the clock to get a plan in place and executed within the next three months. I'm not trying to drag this out for my whole term. I want peace and quiet tomorrow."

"Wow," Troy said. "I'm sorry to hear about your mother—I can't imagine. I feel somewhat better after hearing all of this. Gerald is absolutely known in the community, and we're glad he's by your side—we just wish that it was someone like him in your position. It would create that trust."

"I have a lot to restore," Martin said. "I wish Chris was my only problem, but we have no Council. As fun as it might be, I'm not interested in being the sole decision-maker for the entire organization. We need our checks and balances, or else we're no different from the Revolution."

"I completely agree."

"You never answered my question, Troy. How serious is the push for a recall vote? Do you have the signatures?"

For a recall to be considered, at least two-thirds of the Road Runner population would have to sign a petition pledging their support for the measure. This would then move the matter to the Council for a final decision on holding a formal recall vote or not.

"We've only surveyed a handful of regions so far, but the trends suggest we do have the numbers." Troy lowered his head, avoiding eye contact with the new commander.

"Jesus Christ," Martin muttered, rubbing his forehead. "How am I supposed to get anything done under the cloud of a recall vote?" He turned to Gerald who only shook his head.

"You may be okay," Gerald said. "Even if they get the signatures, there is no Council, no one to review the decision."

"But there will be," Martin said. "At some point. Even still, what does it say to my ability to get anything done if half the membership wants me gone? Basically anything I do will be hated, no matter how good it is."

"Will you excuse us, Troy?" Gerald asked, nodding to the exit. Troy nodded and left the room without another word, his damage done. When the door closed behind him, Gerald spoke again. "Martin, you have nothing to worry about. *You* get to choose the replacement Council members. Just pick people who believe in you."

"I know that—it just seems like a cop-out. I shouldn't have to stack the deck in my favor. If the people really want me gone, then maybe I should just resign."

Gerald let out a long, disappointed sigh. "Ignore these fools. They lost the election and can't bear the thought of it. Don't forget that you received the majority of the votes. More people want you in this role than don't. The negative ones are just being louder right now. Keep your focus, and let's get shit done."

Martin nodded. "Okay. Have they started drilling at all in Alaska?"

"Not yet. We've run into some complications. Chris knows his mansion is safe, so there are always people on his team going in and out of the house, wandering the grounds. Our team is looking for a new, farther out location to start drilling. It may add a couple of days, but I believe we can still reach our target within a couple of weeks."

"Perfect, keep me updated on that. And let's see if we can't stop all this buzz about the recall. Maybe launch a campaign against it."

"I'll see what we can do."

"Thanks, Gerald. I'm really glad you're here. I can't imagine doing all of this on my own."

"Anything you need, Martin. I'll always have your back."

Gerald returned to his office, leaving Martin alone with his thoughts, dreading how long the next two weeks would take to pass.

9

Chapter 9

Sonya Griffiths was trapped in 2064 where she lived in downtown Denver, no more Juice to transport her to other eras of time—a virtual prisoner in the future, forced to hide from the organization she had once loved. She had always known it was a matter of time before someone within the Road Runners connected the dots and tried to take her life. Hell, she didn't blame them one bit. If the roles had been reversed, she would have done the same thing.

It had been an emotional roller coaster watching her friends become enemies. Commander Strike was one of her closest confidants, two strong women running the world, kicking ass and taking names. But it was Strike who had ordered the hit on Sonya, and sent Martin Briar to carry it out.

She didn't enjoy hearing the news of Strike's death, but did think of it as a sort of poetic justice. Strike had found herself in quite the mess, and she'd probably still be alive had she not tried to tango with Chris. But that's not something any commander would ever do. Each new one seemed to push the envelope a bit further, and she could only hope Martin had more sense than to go down that same path.

While she rarely spoke with her father, Chris knew the importance of keeping her alive, letting her live in his down-town Denver residence, a penthouse overlooking the city and mountains, the electric walls keeping all of the lower-class society on the outskirts.

She knew it was wrong, but nonetheless basked in 24/7 security, a driver, a chef, and a maid. Chris even provided a personal concierge. If she needed anything at all, a simple phone call obtained it.

She had utilized this when asking for the Alzheimer's medicine for Martin during his visit into the future. At the time, it was a no-questions-asked policy. And the concierge never did ask a question. But they also kept a log of every request, something that her father had access to and liked to pore over on occasion.

The day after she had given the medicine to Martin, she received a furious phone call from her father. He threatened to kick her out to the streets if she ever helped a Road Runner again, especially Martin. He'd even see to it that she get a one-way trip into the past where it wasn't so easy for her to hide from those hunting her.

She understood loud and clear, but didn't realize that her father would never let this go. That was until the knock on her door from her own security officer, Steve Scott.

"Hey, Steve, is everything okay?" she asked. There had never been any sort of threat to reach the 53rd floor, but she noticed a grave look spread on his typically cheerful face.

Steve was sixty-three years old, a longtime friend to Chris who still had plenty of bounce in his legs. He lived in the same building, and Sonya often saw him working out in the gym during his time off. He lowered his shiny bald head as he reached into the inside flap of his suit jacket.

His green eyes watched her for a moment before he raised a finger over his lips, encouraging Sonya to remain quiet. Her face scrunched in confusion as he pulled out a small piece of paper and handed it to her.

She unfolded the paper and read:

Your father is coming for you, wants to use you to get Briar. Need to run and hide now.

It took her a moment to comprehend the message, but once she did, she looked to Steve with panic swimming in her eyes. He kept his finger held to his lips and gestured for her to hand the paper back over with his other hand. She passed it back before grabbing her purse from the kitchen counter and leaving the apartment without a word. Clearly Steve had a plan, and she was glad to have him on her side. Sonya had always grown close with her father's trusted friends, many of them like family.

It paid off now as Steve wanted to help her instead of being loyal to Chris. She closed the door behind her as they entered the elevator lobby where Steve had already pushed the call button. Sonya fought off the bubbling panic as Steve remained completely silent. It could sometimes take a whole two minutes for the elevator to arrive to the penthouse, but the doors parted with a chime after a few seconds.

They entered and Sonya watched as Steve slipped the note back into his jacket, quickly putting his finger back on his lips once they locked eyes. The tension hung over them like a black rain cloud, the silence a knife jammed into Sonya's sanity. She just wanted an explanation. Was Chris on his way right now? Was she in physical danger? Or was this another of his endless mind games? Anyone close to Chris could attest that they didn't truly know his feelings toward them, let alone his motives.

Steve held his key card to the elevator's panel and held down the "1" button, ensuring them a direct ride without any stops. When the doors parted a minute later and revealed the building's lobby, Steve scanned the area before waving Sonya to follow him toward the exit. They moved at a pace just below a jog until they stepped outside.

"Okay," Steve said.

"What the hell is going on?!" Sonya demanded.

Steve raised his hands as they kept walking away from the building, heading into the bustle of downtown on a weekday. "We're fine—*you're* fine. Your dad is sending a crew to come take you to Alaska in 2020. They were going to tell you some bullshit story about why he needed to see you, only his intent is to hold you hostage to try and lure Briar to his mansion."

"They're coming here now?" Sonya gasped. "How much time do we have?"

"We have time. He sent a crew from Alaska—his finest soldiers. I wanted to get you a head start, and I'll go back to the apartment and play dumb. I'll tell them you went out shopping and that I have no idea when you'll return."

"Where am I supposed to go? I don't have any Juice."

"I know, but you need to get as far away from Denver as you can. I suggest you rent a car and just drive. They'll be out looking for you by nightfall. Be careful out there – the world is a dangerous place outside of the big cities, especially at night. Try to get your travel done during the day, hop city to city, maybe head to the east coast. New York City is plenty busy for you to hide."

Steve kept talking faster with each word, sparking a wave of urgency as Sonya tried to follow along.

"New York?" she asked. "Is it that serious, you think?"

Steve nodded frantically. "Your dad is feeling the pressure of having Briar in charge of the Road Runners. The thought of a Warm Soul calling the shots has sent him into quite the frenzy. He feels he has to end the Road Runners first, or they'll end him. He's desperate and will do anything to stay in control—even use you as bait."

Sonya shook her head. It all sounded made up, but she also had no problem believing any of it. She knew her father was a living monster void of compassion.

"When do you think I can come back? Will he search for me all the way in New York?"

"I think he'll search everywhere, especially since he knows you're stuck in this year. Do you have any friends who can maybe take you to a different year?"

Sonya shrugged. Her only friends were old Road Runners—no one she had spoken with since Martin's half-hearted attempt at killing her in 1996. She had kept a low profile since living in the future, too, not wanting to accidentally expose herself to any potential Road Runners working undercover, waiting for the opportunity to take her life.

"I have no one," she said, dropping her head.

"I wish I could help, but you know Chris will be looking into everyone closest to you to check for any trips through time."

"I know. You'll be one of the first he checks."

"You need to get out of here," Steve said. "Because once they realize you're not coming home tonight, they may close the city—it's that important for Chris."

"Understood," Sonya said, a tear trickling down her face. "Thank you so much, Steve. I don't how to ever repay you for saving me like this."

71

Steve raised a calming hand. "No need. I'm just doing the right thing. No need for you to get tangled in your father's affairs when you're just trying to live in peace. I wish you the best of luck and will be praying for your safety. Go, and don't look back."

Sonya threw her arms around Steve, embracing him for a second, noting the fresh smell of cologne on his jacket. He patted her back and she left without another word, suddenly thrust into a whole new life, survival still her daily goal.

10

Chapter 10

Martin stared into the camera and took a deep breath. It was his first time using the broadcast system that had been installed in his new office. Soon his face would show across devices all around the continent, Road Runners awaiting a much-needed update. He and Gerald had tinkered around with the streaming software, using a quick practice run to ensure they both understood how to use it.

"You ready?" Gerald asked, settling into his seat out of the camera's range.

"As ready as I'll ever be," Martin said. "Here's to hoping they don't storm the building and drag me out."

Gerald chuckled, but Martin wasn't joking. His relationship with the public had already grown tense as of late, prompting him to address the organization to speak for himself, rather than letting rumors define him.

Martin cleared his throat as he clicked to start the live stream, beginning the thirty-second countdown that preceded. Memories from his trip to the future flashed in his mind, mainly the grim reality of what society would one day become.

Unless everyone worked together to save themselves.

The countdown ended and Martin had the organization's complete attention.

"Good evening, fellow Road Runners. This is my first address to the organization, and I want to start by formally introducing myself. I am Commander Martin Briar, and I come to you today to discuss the recent happenings and our plans moving forward."

His arms had been shaking behind the podium, but settled once he was into the thick of his speech.

"The first topic tonight is regarding the attacks on our Las Vegas hotel. Initial investigations have concluded that the attacks were carried out by the Revolution, in combination with the Liberation. As you may have seen in some early news coverage, fires were set on every floor of the building, in the hallways, to provide a distraction and keep people trapped in their rooms. The collapse of the building was due to explosives planted around the hotel. They also drove a double-decker bus into the hotel's main entrance to ensure that people remained trapped inside. This was a deliberate and planned attack that likely took months to prepare. We have no confirmed survivors. This act of terrorism by the Revolution will not be tolerated. My team and I are working every single moment to devise the best plan for retaliation.

"We are down, we are hurt, but do not count us done. For years we've dealt with the Revolution hunting our members, always trying to strike fear into our hearts. I ask you to not live in fear. Be cautious and alert, yes, but there's no need to hide in your homes. We still have a strong organization that can achieve big things, and it's up to all of us members to contribute where we can. There is no better time than now to get involved with your local chapters. There is so much you can do that doesn't involve you risking your life in combat. Something big is coming to the Revolution, and while I can't share the details of our plans, please trust we have the best minds working on it.

"My second item today is to make a call to our Council members. Wherever you are, we need you. I have no intent on passing laws and making decisions on my own. The Council serves as our checks and balances, and has always been a steady presence. I completely understand your reasons for going into hiding, but it's time to get back to work. You're not doing anyone any favors by remaining in isolation. Consider this my official call to you. I'll give you one week to meet with me in my office. If I don't hear from you, I will begin the process for finding replacement Councilors.

"This is not something to take lightly. The Council has long been a collective footprint of past commanders, each one getting to leave a stamp of their legacy on us. If you fail to show up, you'll be entrusting one commander to make decisions that will heavily impact the organization for decades to come. I am no dictator—I have no interest in doing such a thing, but I'm left with no choice should you decide to remain in hiding. We need a fully functioning organization if we ever plan to recover from these dark times. Now is not the time to roll over, but to stand up and accomplish something. I hope to hear from all current Council members regarding their intentions."

Martin paused for a moment to take a gulp of water, his throat parched, before concluding the speech.

"The final topic I want to address is the talk of a recall vote. I completely respect your rights as members to gather signatures, but as a fellow Road Runner I must ask: why are you doing this? You've not even given me a chance to implement changes. I have plans to end this war and save the future, but these things take time. I have a two-year term voted on by the majority of our membership. Had I done something wrong, I'd have no arguments against this, but bear in mind that these attacks in Vegas would have happened regardless of who was in charge. Like I mentioned, they had been planning that for several months, well before I even announced my candidacy."

Martin drew his focus to the center of the camera lens, staring into its soul.

"And Chris Speidel, if you're watching like I know you probably are: your days are limited. You don't get to terrorize our people and hide like a coward. You *will* be punished for your actions. We're coming for you and you know there's nothing you can do to stop me, in particular. I'm not afraid of you or your goons. I've been in your mansion. I suggest you enjoy your final days on this planet because it doesn't end well for you.

"As for everyone else, thank you for your time this evening. I am very much looking forward to working on this recovery effort for our fine organization. Thank you."

Martin nodded to the camera before cutting off the feed.

"How was it?" he asked Gerald.

"Impressive. I didn't think you were actually going to mention the recall vote. Risky, but I think your words will resonate with a lot of our members."

"I guess we'll see if that helps kill the momentum—that's all I'm worried about now."

"I think blowing up Chris's mansion will end any of that talk. People just want action. The timing is unfortunate with the Vegas attacks, the whole mess was sort of dumped on you, but you can recover."

Martin had a phone call with Tony earlier in the week. Even though the campaign was over, Tony still had a wealth of knowledge on the political side of the Road Runners. Tony assured him that the recall vote was a lost cause without an active Council, and even if the votes passed once there was a Council, they would find no justifiable reason to remove him from the commandership.

"I'll be okay. I think you and I really need to focus on shutting out the noise. If people want to talk about recalling me, or just bash me for fun, they can do so—nothing's going to happen, so I don't care."

"You're still going to keep increased security, right?"

"Of course. Chris will be trying to capture me at some point during my term—that much is inevitable. I'm more worried about him than any Road Runners trying to harm me."

"Still need to be careful. Some of our own have left to join the Liberation, and it's mainly the ones who were upset by your victory. If someone no longer feels tied to the Road Runners, they may not be concerned about their ethics."

"I'm always careful, ever since Sonya tricked me. Nothing to worry about on my end."

"Good. We're about two weeks from planting the bombs. We found a spot a quarter-mile away from the mansion and have begun digging. My inbox was flooded after calling for volunteers on this project. People are really excited. We have a crew of almost 200 working around the clock and rotating shifts to keep constant progress."

"And there's no chance of being spotted?"

"None at all. Our entry is out of sight from the mansion and its cameras, and we've set up a campsite even further. We did spot some of Chris's guards in town and decided to not run the risk of staying in the one hotel—not that it would fit all of us anyway. They're digging almost one hundred feet per day. Keep in mind, it's not some massive tunnel we're building, just something big enough to walk through. It will run to all four corners of the house and along its sides. It's quite slick how we have it planned."

"Thank you for giving this all of your attention, and for flying back and forth to make sure it's going well. Have you given any thought to staying in Alaska for an extended time?"

"Not yet." Gerald had already made three trips to Barrow and back, citing a need to assist Martin in Denver until structure was restored within the organization.

Martin nodded. He wanted Gerald nowhere near the site once the bombs were planted. They expected instant retaliation, assuming Chris didn't get pinned underneath any rubble. The whole scene could unfold in pure violence, but Martin would wait to tell Gerald he needed to leave before the bombs were detonated. Perhaps he could watch from the sky if they timed his exit flight just right.

Either way, their main plan was officially in motion, a hopeful end to Chris Speidel's reign of terror now in sight.

11

Chapter 11

Two days later, Martin buckled down on creating a list of potential new Council members, nearly all of them recommended by Gerald or others he trusted within the Denver office. He had met plenty of people during his campaign travels, but lacked the knowledge on whether or not they would be a good fit for the lifetime role.

Every member of the organization kept a public profile that shared all of the missions they had worked on, how long they've been with the Road Runners, and what horrific incident they had to endure from Chris in exchange for their bottles of Juice.

With a list of one hundred potential candidates, Martin had plenty of profiles to sift through, high hopes of weeding the list down to at least twenty finalists to choose from.

It had been thirty-six hours since he delivered his televised message, and still not a word from any of the past Council members. He was about to call it quits on all of them right before his office administrator knocked on the door.

"Commander Briar, Chief Councilman Uribe and Councilwoman Murray are here to meet with you."

"What?! Both of them?" Martin gasped, jumping out of his seat, and dashing out of his office to find the two Councilors waiting with suitcases by their sides.

Thank God, Martin thought. They could have shown up to tender their official resignations, but the suitcases suggested otherwise. And they just happened to be the two most senior members, putting the Council instantly back into strong, trusted leadership.

"I am so happy to see you two," Martin said as he shook their hands. "Please come into my office and let's talk."

They greeted Martin and looked around the bullpen full of Road Runners staring at them like they had risen from the dead.

Once in the office, Councilman Uribe took the seat across from Martin while Murray insisted on the couch.

"I take it you got my message," Martin said as he sat. "Are you guys okay? Where have you been?"

"We did see your message, and thank you for it," Uribe said. "We've been hiding ever since that night. Funny how everything seemed to spiral out of control at the same time. Had it just been the attempted attacks on our chambers, we likely would have resurfaced after a week or so once the chaos died down, but that never happened. It just kept snowballing out of control. The decision to not rescue Strike definitely struck a nerve with the wrong people."

Uribe clasped his hands and leaned back, an elderly man with a life full of wisdom residing behind his eyes.

"And what about you, Councilwoman?" Martin asked, turning his attention to the couch.

"I've had more exciting days, that's for sure," she said. "But I can't complain too much—it was a break from the chambers that I think we all needed."

"Is there anyone else coming?" Martin asked.

Uribe looked over his shoulder at Murray before speaking. "It's just us," he said flatly. "We spent yesterday getting in touch with the others. They all feel it's still too dangerous to resume our work, even though I assured them of the heightened security and remote offices."

"Christ," Martin said, rubbing his forehead. "So we're five short."

"Don't worry," Uribe said. "We are here to assist with this process. You get to choose your candidates, we swear them in and show them the ropes. If you want any advice on who to choose, we can assist there as well—but don't feel like you *need* to check with us."

"Anything you need," Murray added. "Just say the word."

"I appreciate that," Martin said. "I've actually been working on a list of potential replacements and am in the final stages. At this point, I think we'll be ready to move forward next week—just need to conduct some formal interviews to make sure they are all good fits."

"Are you going to tip the Council in your favor?" Uribe asked, stroking his chin.

Martin frowned. "How do you mean?"

"Don't play dumb, Commander. We see the news, and we know there's a lot of people interested in recalling you. With five open seats, you can fill the Council with a majority of members who believe the same exact things as you. Quite frankly, I think it would be irresponsible for you to do anything else."

Martin looked to Murray for reassurance, and she nodded in return. "You can guarantee yourself a peaceful term."

"Well, I've certainly considered it, but didn't want to ruffle any feathers by doing so."

Uribe let out a hoarse laugh. "The feathers are *already* ruffled, Commander. This will just be your way of ensuring it doesn't escalate any more beyond that. I hate to say it, but you're probably the most hated commander in our history, and it has nothing to do with you. We've never been so divided as an organization, never seen so much tension. I don't honestly recall a commander ever being so despised. Can you think of anyone, Councilwoman?"

Murray pursed her lips and shook her head. "No, this is a first. Our greatest fear was becoming political, but that's what has already unfolded once Strike was captured. Even through the worst of times in our past, we were all in it together, so there was never blame to pass around. Our organization has always moved slowly, but forward, and that's the best way to maintain a peaceful membership. The whole Strike matter simply threw a wrench into that steady machine and caused unprecedented chaos and split-second decisions. The blame, unfortunately, falls upon you, more so because you were the one spared for Strike."

"Would you actually vote on removing me?"

Uribe chuckled again. "You haven't done anything. There has never been a recall vote—as I mentioned, purely times of peace. Whatever these people are griping about has no relevance. A recall vote would need to be about your actions as commander, not some grudge about your life before then."

"That's comforting," Martin said, leaning back in his chair as he planted a fist below his chin. "Do you think we'll ever be back to normal?"

"Of course things will go back to normal," Murray said, standing from the couch for the first time. "What we *consider* normal is what will change. After these Vegas attacks, nothing will ever be how it was before. We'll have a more diligent membership because of it, less trust, less desire to be in public places. The organization will have to adjust, host more meetings online and things of that nature."

Martin shook his head. "We can't afford that. Chris has a direct feed into our system. I'm sure he's not constantly monitoring it, but we can't afford to take that risk."

"Well, something needs to change," she replied. "For us, our plan is to no longer work from stationary chambers. We'll bounce around every few months, and plan recesses where we can return home and actually enjoy our homes and families."

"What is your initial plan then?" Martin asked.

"I'll let Councilman Uribe discuss that with you. That was a long trip, and I need to use the ladies' room. Excuse me."

Murray let herself out of the office and closed the door, Martin turning his focus to Uribe.

"Our original plan is to start working here in Denver, and move around every quarter," Uribe said.

"Is that necessary?" Martin asked. "We can expand the office here and give you plenty of room to operate. And we wouldn't tell anyone where you're working from."

"It's necessary. I'm incredibly shaken up by what could have happened to us that night if we weren't tracking that mob of people headed toward our chambers. They would have done to us what they did to that Vegas hotel, no doubt about it. They still may try, but I think the worst has passed at this point in time. I hope."

"I have tons of security. No one gets into this office without approval from me."

"And you decided to let in those protesters? They could have hurt you."

"They were checked before entering. I'm not going to turn away our own members out of fear. I had Gerald in the room with me when I met with them, and more guards standing right outside that door. Besides, I'm a trained machine, don't you know? I can handle a few upset people if they tried anything cute."

"Yes, of course. I forgot about your training before that mission you took into the future. I suppose you are just fine."

Martin nodded as Uribe fell silent, the old Councilman staring into space as he debated his next words.

"Is something wrong?" Martin asked when the silence carried on too long.

Uribe looked over his shoulder to the door before turning back to Martin. "May I speak in confidence?"

"Of course."

Uribe shifted uncomfortably in his seat, leaning on one arm rest as his head remained halfway turned toward the door to see anyone who might appear. "I think Murray was a part of those attacks on us. Possibly even part of the Vegas ones."

"The attacks on your chambers?" Martin asked, frowning. "That makes no sense."

Uribe nodded. "I know it's a heavy accusation, and that's why I haven't told anyone yet. It's absolutely absurd, but I've known that woman for a very long time. The more I think back to that particular day, the less things make sense leading up to us running from the chambers for our lives."

"Tell me about it." Martin's eyes kept dashing to the door.

"She was on her cell phone a lot that day, way more than usual. Both phone calls and text messaging from what I could tell. I noticed her glance around the room numerous times throughout the day, both at all of us Councilors, and to the doors. I thought maybe she was bored or tired—it had been a grueling time for all of us, and I understood that everyone copes in their own way. But later that day, once we realized what was unfolding and headed our way, Murray was eerily calm. Don't get me wrong, she's an incredibly strong-willed person who I've never seen show fear, but the way she sat there and just nodded her head like we were reading news headlines . . . just bothered me."

"Did she say anything during all of that?"

"Sure did. Told us it was likely nothing to worry about. Urged us to stay and get work done, that we were all overreacting. Again, nothing out of the ordinary for her. But I've sat next to her for over two decades in those chambers, and I could just sense something in her tone wasn't quite sincere. She was saying the things she normally would, but it almost sounded scripted."

"What did she do when you all ended up leaving?"

"That's the thing, I made the call for us to leave, but she sort of hung back. I can't actually say if she left the building with us. She was definitely the last one in the room. The more I think back on it, the more the pieces seem to fall into place. Maybe my imagination is running crazy, but she's definitely seemed more distant than she usually is. And she's never been one to shy away when it's just the two of us. I just wanted to bring it to your attention, maybe see what kind of information you can gather without involving her."

Martin leaned forward. "I guess the main question is *why* would she do this? I'm happy to have a team take a look, just to see what might be there. I trust your judgment."

"I'll admit, retirement's been on mind, but no way I walk

away with this much uncertainty. If I were to retire, especially now, she'd become the next Chief of Council, seeing as everyone else will be fresh blood. And if she was running the show that night I don't think any of us would be alive today—except her."

"How sure are you about this?" Martin asked.

Uribe shrugged. "I don't have any actual evidence—just speculation. But something isn't right, I know that much. I think you should at least look into it. And if I'm crazy, then perhaps I will step away for good."

"I can do that. I'll keep you updated, but let's drop the topic for now, she should be back any minute."

They stared at each other in a brief moment of silence before discussing the weather.

12

Chapter 12

A week later, business had resumed as usual; at least, that is what Martin wanted portrayed to the Council and general public. Over that time, five new Council members were sworn into their positions, each one carefully interviewed and selected by Martin and Gerald after extensive discussions. Each new member was vetted on their thoughts regarding recall votes, and each believed that should only be considered if the present commander had done something to put the greater population at risk. Specifically, none believed Martin had done anything to even warrant a discussion.

They decided to choose aggressive candidates to fill the five open spots. Martin's main objective for his term was to bring an end to Chris Speidel, and having a Council backing him every step of the way would prove critical for his entire tenure.

With the new Council in place, they agreed to work in the Denver office, stealing the big conference room as their chambers, for the next three months, at which point they would evaluate what they wanted to do next. Uribe explained the importance of working closely with the new commander while they figured out their own structure moving forward.

Behind the scenes, an early investigation revealed links between Councilwoman Murray and the Liberation. Investigators were still gathering information, a final summary expected by the end of the week.

Uribe decided to remain within the office building around the clock, not so much as stepping outside for five minutes of fresh air. As the investigation uncovered more disturbing truths, he decided his life might be in danger, Murray capable and willing to arrange an assassination on him to propel herself to the Chief's seat.

"When our sessions are over, I'll be in my room," he had explained to Martin after one of their secret meetings regarding the matter.

All conference rooms had been converted to temporary bedrooms for the Councilors.

Today, however, was the first official meeting between the new Council and Commander Briar. The agenda was to simply come to an agreement on proceeding with the attacks on the Alaska mansion.

Martin entered their chambers and shook hands with each member, the room buzzing with excitement as a sense of normalcy started to return.

"Let's get started," Uribe boomed in his authoritative voice.

The Council hushed and sat around an oval table, Martin sitting in a chair to the side of their group.

"Today we have Commander Briar in attendance. It is also our first official session. Councilwoman Murray and I have spent the last few days making sure all of our new members understand our processes and what they should expect on a daily basis for this new line of work. Being our first official day,

I'd like to congratulate and welcome our newest members, for the record."

They all applauded, nodding to each other around the table. Council sessions were always recorded, so Uribe made sure to speak these words clearly into the microphone in front of him.

"Our new members include: Councilman Charles Bolt, Councilwoman Jordan Barns, Councilwoman Victoria Penny, Councilman Patrick Roth, and Councilwoman Lily Dawson. All have been sworn in during a ceremony orchestrated by myself and Councilwoman Murray. All have been appointed to lifetime terms and have the option to retire when they so choose."

Uribe paused to clear his throat and take a sip of water before continuing.

"I'd like to state that we have implemented new rules for these uncertain times. It's safe to say that our lives are potentially at risk for the near future. We are vulnerable to attacks from both the Revolution and the Liberation. Therefore, any Council members who wish to leave the premises must do so with at least two security guards. It doesn't matter if you're just stepping outside for a smoke break – these rules must be followed to assure our safety.

"The second rule I'm implementing is the cease of nonverbal communication between Councilors. Only Councilwoman Murray and I will recall the times where topics were sometimes discussed and fleshed out via email or text message. That is no longer. We know the Revolution has access to our television stream, and we're not sure what else. All official business must be discussed face-to-face. This does not mean they can only be discussed within these chambers. If you and another Council member need to hash out details and want to do it from your own office, you have that right. Does anyone have any questions regarding these rules?"

They all looked around and shook heads.

"Perfect. Now, moving on to the business at hand. Commander Briar had authorized a tunnel to be built to reach the foundation of Chris's mansion in Alaska. The plan is to plant multiple explosive devices on every retaining wall we can reach, four in total. The tunnel's completion is expected within the coming week. As a sign of good faith for the public, Commander Briar is requesting a review of this decision. Let's cast an initial vote to see where we stand. Only a majority is needed to advance, but we will debate the matter if there are less than five 'yes' votes. Please fill in your votes and pass them to the middle of the table."

Uribe had long been a proponent of anonymous voting for the Council, and pulled out a small box for the members to deposit their slips of paper. It only took him a minute to collect all votes and count them out, passing each slip along to Murray for verification.

"Seven to zero in favor," Uribe said. "That was easy. Now for our second vote we are looking ahead. This is all contingent upon actually capturing Chris Speidel. If that doesn't happen, these next few votes we cast are irrelevant. If captured, Commander Briar is asking for a total separation of Chris Speidel's body, into at least twelve different parts, to be stored separately in remote locations around the country. This also assumes we have not found a way to make him mortal, leaving us no decision but to ensure he never roams the planet again. Please cast your votes."

Martin watched them scribble on their slips, only one of the new Councilors, Patrick Roth, showing disgust at the request with his eyes bulged and jaw slightly hung open.

Uribe counted them up. "Six votes to one in favor. Easy again. Final vote is regarding our steps to return to peace. Should we capture and separate Chris Speidel, the commander is requesting we terminate all Revolters and Liberators, by any means necessary, until not a single one exists. Please cast your votes."

This topic caused some stares around the table, and a slight hesitation as the votes took a bit longer to be thrown into the box.

Here comes a discussion, Martin thought, reading the body language in the room. He had a Council who would stop at nothing to get Chris, but the handling of his followers was crossing a different ethical line for some of them.

"Four votes to three, opposed," Uribe announced. "At this time we will discuss the matter and recast votes to see if anyone changes their mind. Would anyone who is on the fence like to open the discussion?"

Murray spoke first. "I don't think terminating everyone is the right move. We should be looking to recruit from them, especially the Liberators, as they were once Road Runners. We can strengthen our numbers while reducing the amount of enemies we have on the streets."

"Councilman Roth, your thoughts?" Uribe asked, his attention on the tall, lanky stick figure sitting next to Murray.

Roth looked up, his Adam's apple bulging, and clasped his hands in front him. "I think leaving anyone on the streets will maintain a threat to our safety. Just a few weeks ago there had been no such thing as the Liberation, and now they're a daily threat to us. Even if the Revolution were to falter with Chris gone, we'll just see new groups forming of those who insist on overthrowing us. Complete termination is the only way to

91

guarantee safety."

"Councilman Bolt," Uribe said, continuing around the table. Charles Bolt was the oldest of the new Council members. The other were in their early thirties or late twenties, Martin wanting them in the Council for many years to come. But Councilman Bolt was sixty-five, and won Martin over with his lifetime of dedication toward helping those who had their lives turned upside down by Chris. He was a psychiatrist with the heart of a public servant. Martin had met with him via teleconference shortly after Marilyn had been killed by Chris, and he grew a deep respect and appreciation for the man. Bolt knew how to be stern and caring at the same time, an ideal attribute for any Councilor.

Bolt brushed back his silvery hair and looked to Uribe from above the glasses perched on his nose. "I agree with Council-woman Murray. These people *can* be converted back to our side. It will take some work, but we can do it. Especially if the threat of war is no longer present—we'd have no need to work under fear and could see to it these people get the proper help they need."

"Councilwoman Barns?" Uribe asked.

Jordan Barns had followed the same course as Arielle Lucila, cutting her teeth on the streets with mission after mission. But she was looking for something less dangerous, and the Council seemed a natural fit on Gerald's recommendation.

"I've seen the future," she said. "We have no choice but to exterminate these people. Even if there are some who are genuine about returning to the Road Runners, the risk of leaving the rest vastly outweighs the reward. As long as one person exists who wants to see our demise, we'll never truly be safe. We must abolish their existence."

"Thank you. Councilwoman Penny, your thoughts please?"

Victoria Penny had long worked in the Road Runners' treasury department, overseeing all financial decisions related to the war.

"We are not a people of committing genocide, plain and simple. While I understand the fear, I can't in good faith vote for the extermination of millions of people, many of which will likely mind their own business as soon as this is all over. I urge those of you who voted to approve to reconsider—we are not monsters."

"Councilwoman Dawson?"

"I voted as opposed. I don't think we need to kill these people or welcome them into our organization. If we just let them be, they will keep to themselves. There wasn't a mass hunt and extinction of Nazis after World War II. They still exist, but are irrelevant in today's society. I believe we are dealing the same kind of circumstances."

"Thank you all for sharing," Uribe said. "I am personally in favor of removing our enemies from society, but am open to debate. I agree with many of the initial points made. This one is tough, to balance our reputation as peacekeepers while considering the safety for all of our members. Perhaps the death of all Revolution members is what will bring the peace. Perhaps we can meet in the middle? We can set up a vetting system to decide who can join the Road Runners, and exile those who don't make the cut. We can also send a message by destroying targeted populations of Revolters, but not all. We can attack their leadership team to leave them truly crippled once Chris is gone. Thoughts?"

"I like the vetting idea," Murray said. "We'd need to outline some parameters on what exactly we're looking for in potential new or returning members."

"I don't know," Roth said. "It seems like a surefire way to get people in our organization who shouldn't be there. They might say whatever they need for us to accept them, but we have no way of knowing their true intentions. We're essentially giving them free insider access to the Road Runners, and I only see that backfiring."

"I agree," Uribe said quickly. "Would hate to see what it's like having an enemy infiltrate and use our own information against us." He stared at Murray while he said this, looking for a reaction that she never gave. He knew it was only a matter of time before they took her out of these very chambers in handcuffs.

She held her gaze on the table in front of her, avoiding eye contact with anyone as she spoke. "We can't barge into people's homes and kill them. We can't drop bombs on communities and extinguish them. If we do those things, then we're no better than the Revolution. Who would you fear more if you were a neutral bystander: the crippled population who just suffered a defeat in war, or us, the people who just keep pushing the envelope to spread death, fear, and chaos?"

Her supporters around the table nodded in agreement, the other two looking to Uribe for their rebuttal. "I think we're in for a long debate on this one. Let's take a ten-minute recess and meet back here to hash this out."

Uribe stood without another word and left the chambers. Only he had the power to call an item to vote, and he planned on dragging this out as long as he could while the investigation continued into Murray's past.

Once all the others stood up, Martin returned to his office to check on the status of that same investigation.

13

Chapter 13

Later that week, just before everyone was set to break for the weekend, Gerald's team of investigators returned with the smoking gun they needed. They had traveled into the past and tailed Councilwoman Murray. There were plenty of instances of her meeting with leadership from the Liberation, either by telephone or in person, but she always seemed to be talking in code with them, like she knew she was being watched.

But she left one hint behind that tied it all together, and it wasn't even her fault. During a breakfast meeting with Thaddeus Hamilton, she had passed over two small slips of paper. One showed the daily schedule for the Council in their New York chambers, and the other was an internal map of the chambers with highlights on particular exits. Thaddeus had slipped the papers under his napkin while they finished breakfast and forgot to take them when they left.

It was such a sloppy blunder that many on the investigating team wondered if the Liberation leader had done it on purpose as a way to eventually out his mole and remove her from the picture.

Whatever the reason, the team swept the restaurant after the two had left, recovering the paper and finding it as the ultimate piece of evidence that tied it all together. There was no diplomatic reason for Murray to have given Thaddeus that specific bit of information. The highlighting of exits further suggested an attack was planned with hopes of not allowing anyone to escape.

The report was written up and sent to Gerald last night, who now briefed Martin on the situation in his office. Martin wanted to bang his head on his desk and wish for it to all end. *Has any commander in history had to deal with so much bullshit during their entire term? Let alone their first month on the job?*

"What do we do?" Martin asked. "I'm not even familiar with this process. Do we have to get a warrant to arrest her? Where do we keep Road Runners in jail?"

Gerald chuckled. "No, this isn't the American justice system. We have clear evidence from a reliable source of investigators. No warrant is needed. You can authorize one of the guards to arrest Councilwoman Murray. We don't have any locations dedicated as jails or prisons—our crime rate within the organization is essentially non-existent. In the past, we've simply converted a room in one of our offices to serve as a confined space until the trial begins. The trial is done by the Council."

Martin snorted at this. "So you're telling me everything we need to do this is all right here?"

"It appears so. The Council runs the trial and delivers the verdict. I serve as a tiebreaking vote if needed, since they will only have six voting members with Murray on the stand. You can authorize this arrest at any time."

Martin checked his watch. It was already 1:30 on Friday afternoon. "Will the Council work over the weekend for this?

Maybe I should just wait until Monday. Do we even have an open room to convert to a holding cell?"

"I'm already on the room conversion—just a matter of switching the locks and knobs so it locks from the outside only. The Council normally takes weekends off, but they are confined to this building and this is a pretty severe case. I wouldn't be surprised at all if Uribe decides to start tomorrow, or even tonight, depending on their workload."

"Is this the right call, having a brand new Council take this on? Uribe will be the only experienced one up there."

Gerald shrugged. "The timing's unfortunate, but we picked the right people for the job. They just need to be jurors, and Uribe will preside as the judge."

"Okay. Let's do it now." Martin's guts twisted at the thought of having a trial for one of his own Councilors on charges of corruption and conspiracy.

"Just need you to put the request in writing and I can deliver it to someone on the security team."

Martin obliged, pulling out a sheet of paper with his name, title, and contact information printed on the Road Runner letterhead. He scribbled a quick note like a doctor writing a prescription and slid it across the desk where Gerald snatched it up and left the office. "Thanks, Boss," he said, nodding to Martin before closing the door behind him.

A guard always remained outside Martin's office door, but Gerald didn't want to pull that one away, heading toward the main entrance instead, where one man and one woman stood on watch. They rotated quite frequently to ensure fresh, rested minds were available for such a critical job in these dangerous times.

"Devin, Randall, how are you two today?" Gerald greeted

them.

They both showed wide grins.

"Good, Lieutenant, how are you?" Devin asked. She stood tall with her tattooed arms crossed in front of her, studying Gerald with curious brown eyes.

"Good, but have had better days. Found out some really disturbing news over this last week, and it's led to this." He handed the paper over to Devin who immediately started reading, Randall perusing over her shoulder as he leaned in.

"No," she said. "Is this for real?"

Randall frowned as he read, eyes dashing to Gerald once he finished.

"I'm afraid so. We were tipped off by a reliable source, and that prompted an investigation. They kept digging and digging and this is what was found."

"Holy shit," Randall finally said, his spiked black hair swaying as he shook his head. "This is a major scandal. Do we need to ramp up more security around the building?"

"Not needed," Gerald said. "The trial won't be open to in-person attendees, but it will be broadcast for everyone to watch."

Normally, anyone could wander into the Council's chambers to view a rare trial, but under the circumstances of the chambers sharing the same building as all of the Road Runner leadership, the Council passed one of many rules to keep the public out of the building.

"Conference room six should be ready for a holding cell, if you can make the arrest now."

They both nodded, Randall reaching to the back of his utility belt for a pair of handcuffs. "Let's do this."

"You want us to go into the chambers while they're in

session?" Devin asked.

"I'm afraid she remains a major threat as long as she is free to roam. We need her in that holding cell as soon as possible. Councilman Uribe should know what's going on, so don't feel bad about letting yourself in."

All three started down the long hallway toward the end where the big conference room waited. Their boots stomped on the concrete ground, clopping like a group of horses. Several eyes from the bullpen followed them, as this was certainly not part of the daily routine. Gerald heard whispering, speculation.

The door into the chambers was closed, the muffled sound of voices audible as they approached. Randall didn't hesitate and opened the door, the roomful of Councilors falling silent as all heads turned to him. The new members watched in amazement, but Uribe nodded with a small smirk.

"Councilwoman Murray," Randall said in an authoritative voice. "You are under arrest for corruption, treason, and conspiracy against the Road Runners. Let's not make this any more difficult than it needs to be."

Murray's eyes bulged as she watched Randall and Devin approach, the glimmer of handcuffs catching her attention. She turned to Uribe on her left. "You son of a bitch! What have you done?"

Uribe held his gaze forward, ignoring his long-time colleague and former friend. Jaws hung around the table as it finally registered with the new Councilors what was unfolding.

"I should have eliminated you sooner, you old bastard!" Murray ranted as Randall smacked the cuffs around her wrists, forcing her to her feet. "If you think this is over, you're wrong. I'll see to it. You better watch your back if you ever take your old ass out of this building. Coward!"

Uribe laughed through his nose at this comment as the two guards started toward the door with Murray between them, disappearing back down the hallway.

The silence in the chambers could have been cut with a plastic spoon. Gerald remained behind and shuffled toward Uribe, addressing the group. "There will be a trial. It's up to you all to decide the start time and terms. Please report to me when everything is in place so I can coordinate with the appropriate parties."

"I know this is a difficult time," Uribe said. "Welcome to the Council. Trials are never easy or fun. I'm sure this one will have some added weight since it's one of our own. I have known Councilwoman Murray for almost two decades, and as right as I know this was to do, believe me that it was a dagger in the heart to watch what just happened. Let's take a thirty-minute break and meet back here to discuss how we want to proceed. Plan on clearing your schedules for at least the next week."

Uribe stood and met Gerald behind him, no one else moving yet. Uribe spoke in a hushed voice. "So it's all confirmed?"

Gerald nodded. "I'm afraid so. They found a rock-solid piece of evidence to tie it all together. Should be a pretty straightforward trial."

Uribe shook his head, disappointment drooped on his face. "I was hoping so much that I was wrong, but here we are. What did Commander Briar think?"

"He was just as shocked as everyone else. I feel for the guy—what a start to his term."

"I know it, but if we can actually pin all of this on Murray and put her away, it will only look good for him. Sweeping out corruption from under the rug has never been a bad thing for any leader."

"I suppose, but right now he's seeing it as another negative on his image."

"None of this is his fault. He literally had nothing to do with this. Tell him I said to relax."

Gerald grinned. "Will do, sir."

"Okay, well I'm gonna step out for a minute and clear my head. It's going to be a grueling trial, especially if she keeps yelling at me like I'm the guilty one."

Uribe nodded to Gerald before turning to leave the chambers where the silence would soon give way to the chaos of a heated trial. Gerald left to inform Martin that all had been taken care of.

14

Chapter 14

While the drama in 2020 unfolded, Arielle Lucila crouched behind a bush in the year 1988, having followed the last thirty years of Chris Speidel's life. Not thirty consecutive years—no one would ever order that—but rather jumping through his past to eventful days in his life. Even as the Keeper of Time, Chris had plenty of days where he never left his house. With his phones bugged, Arielle listened to his morning briefing calls and could usually decide if a day was worth her time.

This particular position of hiding behind shrubbery had become normal since she started following Chris around every waking moment of his past. She had a routine of tailing the old man all day and night on the eventful days, and when he turned in for the evening, she returned to the year 2000 that she had designated as her safe space to jot down notes for the day. She had accumulated a thick binder, tracking all information on Chris since his days before time travel.

Having so many notes suggested an interesting life for young Chris Speidel, but Arielle found those particular years extremely boring – that was until the night she followed him as he carried his dead wife out of the house and tossed her into the trunk of his car like a sack of groceries.

She referred to this as his 'turning point', his first evil deed of many to come. He had lived a rather vanilla life up until this tragedy, but afterwards was when matters snowballed out of control. Within a week of rolling the body down a mountain and into a river, Chris had officially joined the Revolution as an active member.

She watched him evolve from a reserved, minds-his-own-business member to the monster he was now known as. He started doing small jobs for the Revolution, trips into the past to tail people—much like she was doing—returning with information on the subjects in question.

These trips into the past eventually took a dark turn, and she couldn't figure out why. Needing to keep a safe distance, she couldn't always get close enough to hear his conversations with other Revolters. Once he started taking trips into both the past and future, where she typically had to scramble to keep up, and returning with souvenirs from his slashed victims, she began to see the demon being groomed.

She had bugged his phone, hoping to learn who was ordering Chris to do such evil tasks, or at least find out why, but his phone calls only consisted of information regarding his upcoming missions. It was the burning question that kept her up at night. Knowing the reasoning behind what made someone tick was the most valuable piece of information. You could essentially control a person if you understood what motivated them.

She accepted that this answer remained behind one of many closed door meetings that Chris had with Revolution leadership. Her focus was better spent pursuing a means to his death.

She had followed him through his rise to the highest honor in all of time travel, the Keeper of Time. The move was stunning, yet somehow fitting. Chris had certainly paid his dues, working tirelessly around the clock for the Revolution, jumping at whatever they needed help with. Leadership noticed and nominated him for the position before eventually choosing him.

Arielle noted, at this time, that the Revolution was still a rather innocent group of time travelers. Sure, they had authorized some missions that looked bad on the surface, like murdering a well-respected middle school teacher for no apparent reason. But that same murder was done to prevent a future where that same teacher would sexually traumatize ten students in one school year.

The work was dirty, but done with the right intentions. The Revolution remained this way for a couple of years under Chris's new leadership, gradually drifting from meaningful work and toward a massive recruitment force. In his early public addresses, Chris cited the never-ending Vietnam War as a reason for needing a bigger population of Revolters. War could strike at any time, and they needed to be prepared as much as anyone to counter potential attacks.

What Arielle found throughout Chris's life was an obsession with not just war, but the suffering that followed it. He enjoyed entrenching himself in the communities most effected, not to offer the support of his resourceful organization, but simply to observe. This proved true for any and all tragedy. He was drawn to pain and suffering like a moth to light.

Arielle had knowledge in just about every meaningful subject, including psychology. Observing Chris for so long led her to conclusions about him that perhaps no one had drawn before.

104

Before the murder of his wife, he had never shown an interest in tragedy. After that event is when the obsession gradually grew. She concluded that his own tragedy shook him to the point of a mental breakdown. Not only did he lose his wife, but he lost his daughter in the process. Sure, she might have lived with him during her adolescent years, but she was very much checked out from the relationship and wanted nothing to do with her father.

He lost everything in exchange for a new life full of promise and wealth. Arielle supposed he grew this attraction to tragedy as a coping mechanism. Watching other people suffer made him feel better about his own questionable life choices. Perhaps he felt like he had no control, bullied by the Revolution to join and commit atrocious acts. Many of the innocent lives lost in wars also had no choice, victims of their circumstances and nothing more.

Arielle believed this could be used against him, but exactly how was the troubling question. She presumed he had escalated tensions with those who didn't agree with the Revolution, causing the split that became known as the Road Runners, and promptly taking them to war. He had engulfed himself in so much war, that she had to believe he knew exactly what he was doing, orchestrating every move, intentionally sacrificing lives of his own people for a greater purpose. They were at war with a mastermind general and never realized it. He had always managed a facade as a lunatic with no plan, but Arielle was realizing for the first time that he was guiding the Revolution to be the greatest threat to all of society. Chris really could rule the world in due time, a project he had been working on since the beginning of his reign.

"We have to get the Keeper status away from the Revolution," she said to herself many times as she fell asleep each night. The thought of Chris wielding the ultimate powers now frightened her. The world wasn't safe as long as he lived. He had to be killed by any means possible and have his powers stripped and deferred to someone without evil intentions. But who would that be? That amount of power was sure to corrupt even Mother Teresa.

She'd leave that sort of decision for the commanders to bicker over. For now, the main priority needed to be killing Chris. Sonya was the obvious route and should be immediately tracked down. Chris wasn't going anywhere until she was removed from the equation.

Tonight, Arielle was ready to call it a day and head back to her safety zone. She had been hiding behind this bush for two hours, waiting to see if Chris emerged from his house one hundred yards away. He had made no phone calls and only the glow of light from a TV flashed from the visible window. His day was over, but the urgency never died for Arielle. She had debated all day about calling off her mission and returning to Commander Briar with what she had gathered so far. The amount of information should suffice for what they had set her out to do. The longer she stayed near Chris, the more likely she'd be captured, rendering all of this research useless.

I'm going back to 2000 to update my notes, and will call the Commander in the morning. He can decide if I need to stay longer, but I'll urge him to call this off. We have what we need, and I can help on the new mission to kill this monster.

She talked herself into it and pulled her flask of Juice from her back pocket. The Road Runners had been able to reproduce her Juice, giving her a copious amount in the form of twenty bottles once she had become known as their best field agent.

She took the necessary sip and thought of the year 2000 where safety awaited.

* * *

After a long night of tossing and turning, Arielle got out of bed at 6 A.M. and dressed herself for the day, not in her camouflage attire she had been in since stalking Chris, but regular clothes of jeans and a button-up. She even put on a light layer of makeup and admired herself in the mirror. It had felt like decades since she last got dolled up and had an evening for herself. And while true free time would wait a bit longer, she felt like herself instead of the fierce agent she had been propped up as by the Road Runners.

Somewhere behind those hazel eyes was the woman who wanted to order a pizza on a rainy Friday night and watch scary movies until she passed out. In some other dimension her old life continued with her parents alive, her college boyfriend off the streets, and a job she had truly loved as a CIA agent.

These flashbacks often tried to infiltrate her mind, but she pressed forward, believing the past only dragged you down with it. Life had surely been upturned, but her future remained bright. After she had hit rock-bottom, Arielle immersed herself in hard work and education. The CIA was still willing to proceed after a month off work to bury her parents and get her life back into shape, but that was also when the Road Runners approached her and explained the reasoning behind her sudden turn in life.

She had first joined the organization with no purpose, no

goals. Granted, she didn't quite understand the full capabilities of what they were offering at the time, but here she was today, about to place a call to Commander Briar in the year 2020.

She left her motel room, a small truck stop off the side of a frontage road in Colorado Springs. Chris had still lived in the Springs in 1988 where she had last left him, but was gone by the year 2000, off to either New York or Alaska—she hadn't ventured that far enough into his future to know for sure.

It was summer, and the crisp morning air filled her lungs as birds sung from high in the nearby trees, providing a perfect melody for what would surely be a perfect day. Agents were allowed a full week off after completing a mission, but Arielle had parlayed one mission after another for the past three months. She hadn't grown tired until this one in particular, and she planned to spend the free week on a tropical beach where muscular men brought her drinks all day.

A girl can dream, she thought as she pulled out her cell phone. Commander Briar had asked her to communicate all updates directly to him for this particular mission, so she dialed him.

He answered after one ring. "Commander Briar speaking."

"Good morning, Commander," Arielle said. "Do you have a moment?"

"For this mission, I have all the time in the world. How are things? Are you staying safe?"

Arielle rolled her eyes. The organization checked in on her frequently, and she wondered if it was because she was a woman. No one ever checked to see if Gerald was staying safe; they just assumed he was. Little did those same people know, Arielle could bring Gerald to his knees and make him cry. "I'm doing great. Been keeping a safe distance. Bugging the phones really helped. I've been able to work up to 200 yards away when he's home."

"I love to hear that. If there's anything at all you need, please let me know."

"That's what I wanted to discuss with you now, Commander. I've covered a solid thirty years of Chris's life, starting in the years leading up to his joining the Revolution, and am currently in 1988. I feel I've gathered enough information to use—not that there is much to begin with—but it's intel we can work with."

"Thirty years?!" Commander Briar gasped. "I only put you on this mission two weeks ago."

"I know. I have my methods of skipping forward when it's clear nothing is happening or if a risky scenario arises for myself."

"And you're sure you haven't skipped over anything crucial? Tell me what you've learned so far."

"I'm positive. I don't skip anything unless it's clear Chris is just watching TV or reading a book. For starters, as I'm sure you already know, his life is confirmed as linked to his daughter, Sonya. This process occurred when he became the Keeper of Time, and is something all past Keepers have done to ensure a long life beyond the measures of reality."

"Yes, we do understand that bit of it."

"Perfect. Secondly, what most surprised me was his obsession with tragedy. He takes a particular interest in wars, murders, natural disasters—he rarely misses one."

"What do you mean? Is he *causing* these events?"

"No, nothing like that. He simply enjoys witnessing them. He even traveled back to World War II in Hiroshima, just to be in the city when the A-bomb dropped. He knows he's invincible, so why not get a front row ticket to watch everyone else die?

He's a sick man, but well studied on all tragic matters. I'm concerned we could never outsmart him in this war, as he's studied them all extensively and first-hand, even future wars that we've never heard of."

"And how do you propose we use this information against him?" Martin asked.

"Well, for starters, there needs to be a serious discussion around killing Sonya. At the very least we should try to capture her and get Chris's attention that way. I don't get the impression that he's one to negotiate, but if we hold the key to his immortality, then perhaps we can work something out."

"I'm afraid this isn't a matter of peace, Arielle. We need him removed from existence. And suppose we don't ever find Sonya—she's on the run in the year 2064 and no one has seen her in days. What are some other options?"

"If we can't kill him, then we must capture and imprison him so he can't lead. We need to get the powers of the Keeper of Time in our possession. Chris has already done irreparable damage to the world, but more will come if we can't contain him or the line of successors he surely has in place."

"Okay, I have two thoughts on this. We need to create a tragedy for him to watch, one we can control. Second, I think we need to make a move and capture anyone close to Chris. I assume his next move will be to find someone else to carry his invincibility."

"What do you mean, his next move?"

"My apologies. We're moving to blow up his mansion this weekend. We have approval and are just about ready—we've been building an underground tunnel to reach the house's foundation and take it out from below."

"Oh, wow, so we'll be able to capture him already? That's great news."

"Unfortunately not. We'll only be able to capture him if he hangs around. Obviously we have to keep our own people away during the explosion. There will certainly be a fire to put out and local authorities will arrive. It's too risky for us to swoop in at that exact moment and take him away. We will try to track where he goes, but he'll no longer have a home base. We assume he'll try to hop around to different Revolution offices. The closest one to him is in Seattle. We already have eyes around there just waiting."

"Sounds like things are falling into place."

"They are. Tell me one thing, what is your greatest recommendation out of all this research you've done?"

Arielle sighed, knowing it was all a long shot. "Killing Sonya. We have to. It just makes the most logical sense."

"Thank you," Commander Briar replied, a slight tinge of frustration in his voice. "I can only trust your word, which comes highly recommended. If you feel your work is done, please report back to the office in person with all of your findings. How soon do you think that will be?"

"I should be there in an hour," Arielle said, unable to keep a wide grin off her face. Something about following Chris around the clock made her feel like a pig rolling in the mud. But now she was given the green light to get out of the filth and return home.

"I'll see you then."

They hung up and Arielle returned to her room to grab her things and get the hell out of this mission.

15

Chapter 15

"I've been thinking more since we got off the phone," Martin said. Arielle had arrived to the Denver office and met with the commander and Gerald. "No one on the security team is going to like it, but I think it's time for me to get into the game."

"What do you mean?" Gerald asked.

"I've never actually used my Warm Soul for anything productive. Danced around the streets, sure, but that was silly. They've poked me and drawn blood, run tests on my head, all to find a way to replicate this gift to no avail. Dammit, I'm ready to use it."

"What, are you going to barge into wherever Chris ends up hiding and take him away?"

Martin chuckled. "Of course not. I'm not even talking about him. Arielle and I discussed earlier the importance of capturing those closest to Chris. It's possible he may try to inject his blood into someone else he trusts since Sonya hasn't been heard from."

"She's officially on the run," Gerald explained. "I received a briefing from 2064. Word leaked to her that Chris was sending a team to bring her to the mansion. He wants her by his side to ensure his immortality."

Martin smirked. "It means he knows we're coming. Why else would he worry?"

"True, but it's also a mistake to have her by his side. She's the designated survivor."

The thought of a dead Sonya still infuriated Martin. "Who leaked the word to her?"

"Haven't heard yet. They're supposedly interviewing those closest to her. She had drivers, security teams, maids, chefs. It's only a matter of time until they find out. Have mercy on whoever's soul that it is."

"So she's really gone then?" Martin asked, simultaneously disappointed and relieved.

"I'm sure she'll resurface when this is all over—which it will be. But tell me about your thoughts for capturing Chris's cronies."

Martin laughed. "I like that. Chris's cronies. Arielle, have you thought about this further?"

"Yes," she said. "I'm willing to help, but the first thing we need to do is track down who these people are."

"Duane Betts," Gerald said. "He's been the number two to Chris for as long as I can remember. He's probably the most important one to track down, but I'd assume he's in the mansion with Chris, so he may be a casualty when we blow the place up."

"Chris has an assistant named Mario," Martin said. "He approached me when I was new to all of this. I tried returning to the Wealth of Time store and it was gone. Mario met me—expected me—and told me he worked with Chris."

"Okay, so those are two names to look into," Arielle said.

"Do we know of anyone else?"

"Victor?" Gerald asked. "His counterpart in Europe."

"I don't think they're that close," Martin said. "Actually, I think Chris hates him, just one more person in the way of letting him rule the world. Remember, not all Revolters around the world are bad. Chris has done a serious number on the ones here in North America."

"We'll look into it," Arielle said. "We can get some more agents to tail him for the sake of learning who he visits with the most. I can already tell you from my thirty years I just spent jumping through his past, he keeps an extremely tight circle. It's rare to see someone come into his life and stay. Duane is one I can confirm, but I hadn't seen anyone named Mario through 1988. He must come later."

"He keeps a lot of those soldiers nearby, too," Gerald said. "All of those who live in the mansion with him. Surely he's bonded with at least one of them. Even if not, I doubt it's a stretch to imagine he's bribed one of them to take an injection of his blood and go live on an island somewhere safe. He could essentially live forever that way."

"Do you want to lead this mission, Arielle?" Martin asked. "You already have the experience of tailing him, we would just need some more agents to spread out across time to see who Chris spends his time with."

"How urgent is this?" she replied. "I've worked three months straight, and was hoping to get away for a week."

"Three *months*?" Martin gasped. "Yes, please take a week off. Gerald can take this. We have all of your notes and can review those. I'm not even sure what to expect in the coming days. We have the explosion most likely on Sunday, and the start of a major trial on Monday. I know we have the resources, it's just a matter of getting things in motion."

"I already have the right people in mind for the job," Gerald said.

"Great," Martin said. "Get your rest, Arielle. Unplug from all of this. When you're ready to come back, let me know. I want to look into these special teams that used to venture to different times to change things. That's what this organization was started for and we've been pulled away from meaningful work thanks to Chris and his manufactured war."

"I'd love that, Commander," she replied with a wide grin. "I used to be very involved with those missions, still am from time to time, but lately everything has been about the Revolters, and now the Liberators. I just want it to all end and get back to business."

"We'll be there soon enough," Martin assured. "Any final thoughts before you start your well-deserved vacation?"

"Yes," she said. "I'm going to give it a try, even though I already know how you feel. Commander, it's urgent to put your feelings aside for Sonya and look at the big picture." Gerald shifted in his seat, knowing how much Martin absolutely despised being told that Sonya needed to die. "Gerald and I have both spent extensive time in the future. I've now seen the foundation of the man behind that grim future. It's simply not worth it to *not* sacrifice one person for the sake of humanity. We encounter a genocide in the future where millions of innocent lives are lost—some of those close to Gerald. That is the only reality he's ever known. Let's give him a different outcome. You've seen the future – I don't need to explain it to you. This can be stopped. Do the right thing, make the gut-wrenching decision, and commit to saving humanity as we know it."

Martin's lips were pursed as he listened, and he slowly

nodded his head. "Thank you, Arielle. I will consider this. Is there anything else?"

His tone came out dismissive and Arielle understood she was beating a dead horse. "No, sir, that is all. Thank you for your time today."

"Hey," Martin said as Arielle stood up and started for the door. "Thank you. You did phenomenal work on your mission and we have a lot to consider. Enjoy your time off, and I don't want to see you until you're completely refreshed."

"Thank you, Commander." Arielle smiled before turning to leave the office, and Gerald followed her out to the hallway.

"Don't be discouraged," he said. "That was the most receptive of a reaction I've seen him have about Sonya."

"*That* was receptive?"

Gerald chuckled. "Believe it or not, yes. Your words struck something inside. You got through to him, and now we'll see if that actually changes anything. But I wanted to reiterate our thanks for your work. You *have* changed the future of this war – now we need to get to work and figure out how to go about this. Keep an eye on the news while you're on vacation because we might be moving fast once that mansion goes down."

"Will do. Do you think he's serious about the new missions? The more fun ones?"

"He absolutely is. He loved the concept. I have a feeling he's going to actually end this war. Win it? I don't know. But I sense it's going to end one way or another during his term. We've never had a commander just go for it like he is. They've always danced around the thought of attacking Chris, worried about what the retaliation might be like. It can be devastating, yes, but Chris seems concerned."

"And he keeps blowing us up."

"Exactly. If we do nothing, he'll eventually kill all of us. That might have been Chris's plan all along, a slow and steady extermination. But he's forced Martin's hand. Of all the commanders to piss off, he chooses the one who can resist the freezing of time."

"Are you really going to let him risk his life to capture these people?"

"*Me?* He's the commander. I don't have any control over what he does. The Council can technically order him to stay out of the line of battle, but someone would have to inform them first of his intent. I'm not going to, and neither are you."

Arielle nodded. "Are you going to go with him?"

"I can't. We can't both be at risk. There needs to be a successor in case things go south. He'll be fine, though. He held his own in the future—I'm not worried."

"I hope you're right. We've all been through enough with Strike."

"I have no doubt that Martin will come out of this thing looking like the best thing to ever happen to the organization. He has a good heart and genuinely cares about everyone's safety. He recognizes that no one is truly safe until Chris is dead."

"Then why can't he wrap his head around killing Sonya?!"

"I know. I want to strangle him sometimes, he's so stubborn about that. But I suppose that's what love does to a man. Fear causes irrationality, but love stirs it beyond comprehension. Just give him time, I'm still working on him as much as I can."

"Well good luck with that," Arielle said with a smirk. "I really should get going. The beach is calling."

"Have a margarita for me. Stay safe, kid."

They high-fived each other and Arielle left an office that

would never be the same once she returned.

16

Chapter 16

On Monday morning, Martin entered the Council's chambers still fuming from the phone call he had received the previous day. The team in Alaska had informed him they needed two more days to complete the setup around the mansion, citing some complications they had encountered as they approached the structure from underneath. Everything was under control, they had assured him, but the extra time was essential to completing the project correctly. Every day with a team out there digging made Martin nervous, increasing their chances of being caught by the crazy old man and throwing all their hard work out the door. They had no time for delays, but fate didn't seem to care. Tuesday morning was now set on the calendar for the planned demolition.

Instead of worrying in his office all day, Martin and Gerald decided to watch the trial in the Council's chambers. Uribe predicted a swift trial, taking no more than Monday morning, after reviewing the initial evidence presented to him by the investigation team. The Road Runner justice system had no attorneys to try and spin the truth and weasel their way out of obvious guilt. Evidence was presented and the defendant had the right to explain themselves. Uribe suggested there was nothing Murray could say to plant so much as a grain of doubt in their minds. The longest part of the trial would likely be the Council's closed-door discussion regarding her sentencing. They refused the death penalty, the severest punishment likely Murray being exiled to one of their remote islands reserved for such criminals.

The Road Runners owned many uncharted islands in the Caribbean, Antarctica, and Polynesia. A handful were used to store military supplies, but many remained abandoned, their purpose to hold prisoners of either the Road Runners or the Revolution.

Murray was led into the chambers, hands cuffed in front of her, promptly at 8 A.M. Around the clock news coverage had slowly resumed over the last week for the Road Runners' internal streaming channel, and they vowed to air every minute of the trial. A couple of news anchors and their camera operators were the only other attendees in the chambers aside from Martin and Gerald.

The room had been rearranged for the trial. Gone was the oval table the Council normally sat at, replaced by a straight one facing two smaller tables where Murray sat opposite the lead investigator who had busted her.

The Council filed into the room dressed in long black cloaks that were only worn during a formal trial, as they now served as the jury and judges.

"Our trial is in session," Uribe announced in a booming voice, taking his place in the middle seat. Everyone had notebooks they opened across the table once they were seated, pens clicking as they prepared for the trial ahead. "Everything I say after the words 'Our trial is in session' will be on the record until I deem the trial in recess or complete. I ask for you media folks to respect that and not record anything if we are formally off the record. That's not to say you can't speculate and report the happenings during that down time, but no camera footage or audio should be broadcast. Are we clear?"

The two reporters nodded.

"Perfect. You may also hear me say things that sound out of place, but I'll just be speaking particulars that need to be recorded, as our official record is audio only. I may need to describe the happenings around the chambers to ensure a clear picture for our records.

"Now, our trial is in session. Councilwoman Jill Murray, please stand for the reading of your official charges."

Murray stood and rolled her eyes. Apparently her bitterness toward Uribe hadn't worn off since Friday.

"Councilwoman Murray, you are being charged with conspiracy against the Road Runners for colluding with a known enemy group called the Liberation. You are being charged with corruption and abuse of your role as a Councilor, endangering the lives of your fellow Councilors, and threatening the well-being of our membership. You are being charged with treason. All three of these charges will carry their own verdict and sentencing. Do you understand your charges?"

Murray grinned, but did not speak.

"I'll take your smile as confirmation. Please be seated."

Murray sat, a smirk stuck on her face.

"Our trials are very straightforward. We will hear first from the lead investigator who worked this case, then from Councilwoman Murray. After both sides have spoken, the Council will convene in private to discuss a potential verdict and sentencing, or if we'd like to hear more information. Any member of the Council can ask a question at any time. I also want to take this moment to address the fact that, beside myself, our entire Council is filled with new members within the last month. Rest assured, I spent time individually with each member over the weekend to ensure they are up to speed with our trial process and that they are comfortable with their role. I am confident we are a team ready to make unbiased judgments in this trial, despite the defendant being a Council member. Mr. Jay Godwin served as the lead investigator for this particular case. The floor is yours."

Jay Godwin, a 45-year-old Black man, rose from his seat, buttoning his pinstriped suit before flipping through an open binder on his table. "Thank you, Chief Councilman." He slid on a pair of glasses and looked down to his notes, the bright lights of the chambers glaring off his bald head. "This case came across my desk last week and my team immediately jumped on it. We tailed Councilwoman Murray for a timeframe dating back exactly one year to make sure we didn't miss any potential evidence. In December of 2019, we discovered the Councilwoman starting to have an increase in phone calls to a particular number that we were able to trace to Thaddeus Hamilton, the leader of the Liberation. Due to laws in place, we were unable to listen to the calls of a Councilor, but we do have records showing these calls were placed.

"After we discovered these calls, we sent out more agents to tail Mr. Hamilton. We were able to get one of our own to join the Liberation as an undercover spy. They have fairly lax qualifications to join their group, and we had our insider planted a week after the discovery of the first phone call. During this time, the Liberation's only topic of discussion was regarding the extermination of the Road Runners' Council and chambers. This obviously raised some red flags, as we understood a member of our own Council was in daily contact with the man planning this attack.

"The phone calls continued for two months, and eventually led to an in-person meeting between Mr. Hamilton and Councilwoman Murray at a diner in New York City called the Railway Diner. We watched from afar, with agents both outside and inside trying to hear the conversation. We had no luck in gaining information this way, but when the two left, we swept their table and found this."

Jay held up the infamous sheet of paper that was a map of the Council's New York chambers.

"This is a map of the chambers with all exits highlighted. On the backside were handwritten notes of the Council's daily schedule. We compared the handwriting to Councilwoman Murray's. Our forensics team determined the two as an exact match. I have the forensics report available for you to review.

"This one piece of evidence made it very clear what was going on. After sitting down and combining all of the evidence we had gathered, we arrived to the conclusion that the phone calls between Councilwoman Murray and Mr. Hamilton were part of a grand scheme to remove all Councilors from the Road Runners. With the Councilwoman knowing the attacks were coming, she would have survived and been the only remaining member, automatically becoming the next Chief Councilor. As we know, the Council members from that night of the planned attacks all survived, but decided to remain in hiding for fear of their lives. The chambers were still burned down and sent a ripple through our society that caused a continent-wide shutdown of our operations. That concludes our report of the investigation – thank you."

Jay returned to his seat while all Councilors finished jotting notes.

"Councilwoman Murray," Uribe said. "You may stand and state your defense."

Murray rose, her expression bored. "I'm afraid I can't offer much in response. Even if I stood here and said this is all a lie, none of you would believe me. What I really want to know is who was the rat that sparked this investigation. Was it you?"

She fired her question directly to Uribe who started shaking his head. "Councilwoman, this is inappropriate for your defense, and completely irrelevant."

"I don't give a *shit*. I've been in a holding cell for the last three days—I demand to know who is responsible."

"Suggested by the evidence, *you* are responsible, Councilwoman. Now do you have any actual defense for these actions? Something concrete for us to consider."

"Yes, I think it's irresponsible for the investigators to jump to conclusions about my meetings with Mr. Hamilton. There is no actual proof that shows me involved with the attacks the Liberation carried out that night. There's not even so much as hearsay, just a leap of faith that connects me to a map. If this is all it takes to send a Road Runner official to prison, then the organization has a corrupt future ahead."

"Then what was the purpose of the map? Please do share."

"Mr. Hamilton was inquiring about building his own chambers for his newly formed Liberation. He wanted an idea of our layout. The schedule on the back was shared to give him an idea of what we do on a daily basis."

"And it's a coincidence that this same man arrived to our chambers less than a week after this meeting? With hundreds of his followers ready to burn the place down with everyone inside. I may be old, Councilwoman, but my memory is still sharp as a tack. I remember that particular night. You kept pressing us to stay, told us there was nothing to worry about regarding the hundreds of people gathering in our parking lot at the most random time of day."

"There was nothing to worry about. You all overreacted. I don't know what those people were there for."

"They burned our building to the ground, in case you forgot. *That's* what they were there for, and you wanted us inside while it happened."

"My point exactly: you're drawing your own conclusions."

"I think we've heard enough, Councilwoman. The writing is on the wall. An innocent person would offer facts and not their own speculation. And they certainly wouldn't try to spin the story in a different direction. This trial will now be in recess as the Council discusses a verdict and possible sentencing, if found guilty. Everyone please leave the chambers until I call for your return. Thank you."

Uribe clasped his hands in front of him and waited for the chambers to clear, Murray burning her gaze into him while two guards escorted her from the room.

17

Chapter 17

Sonya had been on the run for the last week, driving until she no longer could. She had arrived in Washington, D.C. three days ago and had already secured a new apartment on the outskirts of town. She wore tattered clothes in an attempt to blend in with her new surroundings. Surely Chris wouldn't check any of the rundown neighborhoods, seeing as Sonya had millions in her bank account. Because of that, she had the luxury of staying inside of her apartment all day, only leaving to buy a moderate amount of groceries.

Her neighbors shouted at each other all day and night, and a chorus of gunshots kept her awake well past midnight more often than not. Her world, as she knew it, was over. Gone were the days of strolling through downtown, designer purse slung over one shoulder, shopping bags over the other. No more fine dining in the city, no more penthouse suite overlooking the Rockies.

Her life had been reduced to one of simplicity: cook, clean, read, and sleep. She was off the grid, refusing a cable or internet bill, paying for rent and utilities with cash. For being outside her comfort zone, Sonya felt safe for the first time since Steve had informed her people were coming to take her back to Chris in Alaska. She had always known it was a matter of time before Chris made this request. She often thought back to the day that changed her life, when her father had his own blood injected into her body for this archaic ritual deemed necessary for the Keeper of Time. It put her through some depressing years knowing that she was keeping such an evil man alive, but the situation was out of her control.

Her new apartment reminded her of college: living in a dorm on campus, ordering pizza every night, and washing it down with all the beer she could find. Those nights had also consisted of cutting her wrists in hope of letting some of her father's blood out of her body. She had thought doing it enough might clear her system and one of the attacks on Chris's life could finally work.

Yet here she was, living in a place she would have never chosen under her own circumstances, cowering away from public gatherings, settling into her new life of isolation.

"The sun will come up again," she had told herself dozens of times during her cross-country journey, and she said it again every night before falling asleep. She had plenty of time to reflect on her life and wondered how things might have played out had she never joined the Road Runners. If she had stayed by her father's side instead of joining his biggest enemy, she may very well be in a position of power within the Revolution today. She could have become a rich snob like the rest of the upper echelon she often watched her father mingle with. They were all sick, selfish people who wouldn't hesitate to step on your throat if it meant elevating their status, especially in front of Chris.

She had always kept her distance after witnessing her mother's death, but during her teenage years Chris had started attending, and sometimes hosted, these particular gatherings of the Revolution's high class. All the people dressed in fancy suits and sparkly gowns—this was also when Chris started to wear his signature all-black suit. They drank champagne, showed off their flashy jewelry, and bragged about their financial portfolios. Fancy foods were served on silver platters, and it wasn't quite until Sonya reached tenth grade that she realized her dad was living the high life.

He had her wear a dress, although none of hers sparkled like the ones the other women wore at these events. Her father always put on a fake smile and let out fake laughs she had never heard before. He had promised her a life where she could have anything she wanted, and now that it had arrived, all she wanted was to get away from him.

Chris had changed from a loving father to a man who only cared about himself and what others thought about him. Public perception dictated how he acted and dressed, and even how he treated Sonya. During these gatherings he liked to send Sonya to grab beers for his friends, despite having a full staff of waiters available. She was his obedient little puppy, and how they laughed each time she returned hugging six bottles of beer in her embrace, balancing so as to not spill a drop.

Sonya quickly learned that hate was not an emotion, but rather a formed decision. She *hated* Chris. He had ruined her life, shredded her teenage years to pieces, and laughed his way to the top of his bullshit organization. She *hated* that his life was tied to hers. The thought of suicide popped into her mind on occasion, just for the satisfaction of knowing what it meant for her father.

The Road Runners had provided her a home, all of the members having their lives somehow ruined by Chris. She connected with them, understood their struggles perhaps better than anyone else. They were reluctant at first, but eventually welcomed her with open arms. Gone were the days of being a social outcast. She made new friends and formed new memories, even working her way to the top of the Road Runners, becoming Commander Strike's most trusted recruiter.

She often wondered what life would be like had Strike never made the decision to try and take Sonya's life. She was still shocked that they would turn on one of their best members, but understood why. The secret had stayed locked up long enough, but it was only a matter of time before someone tried to use the connection between Sonya and Chris to end the madman's life.

It all led to her in this run-down neighborhood in D.C. today, surviving one day at a time. Somewhere in the world Chris was on the hunt for her, as was her old friend and former lover, Martin Briar. She couldn't help but wonder what life would be like had she taken up Martin on his offer to run away together. Instead, she was trapped in 2064 by her own fault.

"How stupid was I?" she asked as she lay on her living room couch, staring to the ceiling fan than spun in a hypnotic trance. She had plenty of decisions to dwell on from her storied past, but none of it mattered or contributed to her survival. She now lived day to day, staying off the radar as she tried to brainstorm a plan for a new life.

All of her resources were gone. Chris controlled everything the Revolution could offer and she wouldn't dare endanger any of the friends she had, much like Steve had voluntarily done by getting her out of Denver as quickly as possible. The Road Runners might offer her support, especially with Martin in charge, but she could never fully trust them again. There would always be an underlying chance that they'd turn on her.

She didn't fear for her life, but only worried about being picked up from either party trying to further their agenda. All communication to the outside was cut off, leaving her with screaming neighbors to potentially converse with. Maybe they were nice people just struggling to get by.

"I'll be fine," she said, rolling onto her side for a glimpse out the window. Her apartment was on the second floor, facing west, and she only opened her blinds when the sun shone directly through after three o'clock until sunset. The world looked so massive through that window, Sonya a mere speckle of dust in the vast universe. And when the neighbors weren't yelling or throwing dishes against the shared wall, she listened to the stillness and silence the world had to offer. Even in her rather remote lifestyle in the big city, Sonya had never stopped for a moment to realize just how chaotic life was.

She lounged in her new dwelling, not in fear, but in appreciation for taking a step back and having a second to catch her breath. Surely the hunt for her would resume at some point in the future, but she'd be rested and ready.

Chapter 18

Everyone filed back into the Council's chambers at 2 P.M. Uribe had announced the resumption time at noon, citing a decision had been made, but wanted to give everyone a couple hours for a lunch break.

Martin ordered pizzas for the entire office and encouraged everyone who wasn't already, to watch the delivery of the verdict for this critical time in Road Runner history. Martin used the extended break to make phone calls to potential replacement candidates for the Council. The information was still fresh from his last round of interviews and he already had particular folks in mind.

It was impossible to replace Murray's almost two decades of experience, and with the Council already leaning overwhelmingly in Martin's favor, he decided on a gentleman by the name of Yohan Templeton, his opponent in the election for commander.

Templeton had drastically different views compared to the rest of the Council, and Martin hoped it would bring some balance and perspective during their many discussions on the state of the organization. This was, of course, all contingent on Murray being found guilty and removed from her position, and if Templeton would even accept such an offer.

It was a crazy move on Martin's part, but one that just might win over the segment of members who still seemed to hate him. What better way to move forward from this ugly moment in their history than with the support of the entire membership?

He settled into his seat with Gerald by his side, the room falling silent as Murray entered, the Council following behind.

Uribe was either drawing out the tension to drive Murray mad, or actually needed to sift through the same stack of papers a dozen different times. Eventually he called the trial back into session.

"Councilwoman Murray, please stand for the delivery of your verdict."

Murray stood. She no longer had a smart-ass smirk plastered on her face, instead appearing reflective and a bit scared. Perhaps the reality of the situation had finally sunk in over the break. She had no way out of this, and only a long future ahead to look back on her decisions with regret.

"Councilwoman, do you have any last words to offer the Council before I read your verdict?"

"I only wish to know the name of my accuser," she said in as flat of a tone as she could muster.

"Thank you, Councilwoman. The Council has met with its six available members to determine a verdict in this case. For the charge of conspiracy against the Road Runners, the Council voted six to zero in favor of guilty. For the charge of corruption, the Council voted six to zero in favor of guilty. For the charge of treason, the Council voted six to zero in favor of guilty. This was a unanimous decision across the board due to the evidence presented and your rebuttal. As for punishment, the Council voted five to one in favor of lifetime exile.

"You will be sent to one of our remote locations where you will live on the island by yourself. You will be given a survival kit of shelter, clothing, and hunting gear for food. A team will check on you once a year until you are found dead, but will not offer any support. You are free to attempt to swim off the island, but please know the next closest island is over fifty miles away. Should you somehow manage to make your way back into society and are discovered, you will be immediately sent back to a different island. You are hereby relieved of your duties as a Councilor and shall be stripped of your title. Your flight leaves tonight and you'll arrive at your island within the next twenty-four hours. Prepare for a long trip in the airplane's undercarriage to eliminate any chance of you knowing where you're going. All of your property and possessions will be turned over to the Road Runners for redistribution to the membership, or destruction, depending on necessity. Consider your life as you know it, over. Do you have any questions regarding these terms?"

Murray stood like a statue, tears streaming down her face.

"Very well, then," Uribe continued. "Please see *Miss* Murray out of the chambers and to her holding cell."

Everyone watched as the two guards led her out, Uribe waiting until the door closed behind them.

"This concludes our trial. I want to say thank you to the Council for their hard work on this matter, and I hope they never have to deal with such a crime again. Commander Briar has informed me that he'd like to address the membership, and since we already have the cameras rolling in here, I will offer him my seat for his speech. The trial is now adjourned."

Uribe stood and left the chambers without another word, not bothering to wait around to see what Martin had to say. This had been a grueling process for him, and sentencing someone he considered a friend to a life in exile was surely taking its toll.

All eyes in the room turned to Martin making his way to Uribe's central seat. The rest of the Council remained in position, gawking at the organization's leader as he sat down among them and folded his hands on the table.

"We have had rough times these past few weeks," Martin said to the cameras. "I want to first thank Chief Councilman Uribe for leading a swift trial, and the rest of the Council for stepping up when we most needed it. This was a horrific event to learn about, and I'm glad we were able to deliver justice before Ms. Murray caused any further damage to our institutions.

"I want to take this moment as an opportunity to encourage you all to remain active with your local chapters. What we witnessed was the power of just one person able to shut down our entire organization for months. Do not fear stepping out of your house. We were suffering in the night, but the sun has risen. Return to your lives, celebrate with family and friends, and most importantly, remember to be kind to each other. We will be looking into further measures we can take to prevent something like this from happening again. Our Council members are carefully vetted, yet we have no way of predicting how a position of power will change a person. Ms. Murray served on the Council for seventeen years, and while her reputation is rightfully tarnished, let us rejoice in the fact that she had once worked tirelessly to improve the lives of Roads Runners across the continent. May her legacy be a grim reminder of the drastic swings a person can experience.

"We're at a tipping point as an organization. Tensions are high after the Las Vegas attack, but rest assured that we are close to something big. Something that will change the course of our future forever. Return to your lives, stay diligent, and keep an eye on your neighbors. Until next time, keep safe. Thank you."

Martin nodded to the cameras to cut the feed and they promptly did so, turning to the reporters by their side who immediately started their recaps of the day's events.

"Good speech," Gerald said when Martin returned from shaking hands with all of the Councilors.

"Thanks. Are we for sure ready for tomorrow?"

"I spoke with the team this morning. They said it'll be ready. Some additional digging is being completed tonight, then they'll plant the bombs. They have made a request, though."

"For what?"

"One missile to launch."

"A missile for what?"

"Under our original plans they believed they had a way of funneling some explosives higher in the mansion's structure, but that was part of the complications they ran into. Everything is blocked solid and requires drilling that would surely be heard by anyone living in the mansion."

"Jesus Christ, they're requesting this at the last second? What happens if I say no?"

"Then the plan is off. Understand they were working off the blueprints we were able to obtain. There were some additions underneath that weren't part of the initial drawings, things we would have never seen until getting this close in person. We can still detonate the explosives where they'll be, but it will merely rattle the house and possibly make it sink a bit inward. If we

135

can strike a missile in coordination with the explosion, the mansion will vanish in a matter of seconds. And it guarantees harm to anyone on the second floor, where we know Chris spends most of his time."

"Okay, let's do it," Martin said begrudgingly. He understood that plans could change without notice, but the constant flow of shit he seemed to be dealing with was straining his sanity.

"I'll call it in. I'm thinking one round for a bazooka will be the best bet – we don't need anything much bigger than that and it will be easier for the team to lug around."

"I fully trust your decision... whatever you think will make this happen. I just want Chris out of that mansion by tomorrow night."

"He will be, and then the chase is on."

"Well, the *tailing* is on. I want to capture his friends first. Were you able to find anything on Sonya."

Gerald shook his head. "Afraid not."

"You don't suppose she came across more Juice somehow?"

"I wouldn't rule it out as a possibility, but it's highly unlikely. Her only sources of additional Juice are Chris and the Road Runners. If she was in contact with either we'd know about it."

"Dammit, we really need her. Can you imagine if we had everyone close to Chris in our possession? Checkmate. He'd have no choice but to do whatever we ask."

"Let's not get ahead of ourselves. Nothing is predictable with that man. Even if that scenario played out, I'm sure he'd have another trick up his sleeve. There's a reason this war has gone on this long, and why he's never been captured. That's also why you're reluctant to approach him after we send his mansion into the sky."

"I will never intentionally sacrifice the life of a Road Runner.

They're not toy soldiers; they are real people who contribute to the well-being of our organization. I know you're a military expert, but please understand this is what I believe. Sending anyone toward that mansion immediately after the explosion is reckless. Now, if we find an opportunity, I'm happy to take it – I'm just not going to bet my money on Chris hanging around."

"Fair enough. I've requested a live feed of the attacks tomorrow, something that can only be streamed to your office. We can get some popcorn and enjoy the show."

Martin smirked. "Sounds good. Tomorrow is a new chapter in our history."

And it would be, one way or another.

19

Chapter 19

Martin grew antsy over Monday afternoon. Upon deeper thought, he didn't want the Alaska mansion to explode without at least one of Chris's henchmen in his possession. They already had an available holding cell in the Denver office – might as well put it to use. After a brief discussion with Gerald, and a quick phone call to Commander Blair in London, Martin boarded his private jet at 6 P.M., bound for Fort Myers, Florida.

It wasn't difficult to find Duane Betts, seeing as he had booked a flight to Florida through a regular airline. A quick search connected his mother to the retirement city and they were able to pinpoint an address, kicking into motion an easy mission for Martin to grab Duane and drag him back to Denver.

As much as he would have preferred support with him during the trip, there was nothing anyone could offer, with the exception of Chris Speidel. Once time was frozen, Martin would be on his own.

The jet touched down at eleven o'clock, the night completely abandoned by the retired folks living in Fort Myers. There wasn't exactly a nightlife scene like Miami, especially on a

Monday night. If all went well, Martin would be back on the jet within an hour, Duane by his side en route to Denver.

"All set, Commander Briar?" the pilot asked as the door opened to a flight of stairs. An idle town car waited below.

Martin patted around his body, checking for his cell phone and fully-automatic pistol. Time would be frozen, so he had no intent on using the gun, but it was better to be protected seeing as he was the new leader of the Road Runners.

"I'm ready. I'll see you in a little bit. Keep the engines ready to takeoff."

"Yes, sir." The pilot nodded to Martin as he descended the stairs.

The town car's driver exited the vehicle, leaving the door propped open for Martin. He stood tall in a fine black suit, white gloves on his hands, with a wide, welcoming grin. "Commander Briar, it's an honor. My name is Gregory White. Are you sure you don't need me to drive you around? It's no issue at all."

No one aside from Gerald and Commander Blair knew that time was about to be frozen, nor did it matter. Once it was, everyone else in the world simply froze, their minds unable to process what was happening, resuming as soon as Blair unfroze it.

"It's really okay, young man," Martin said. "They haven't let me drive a car since I became Commander, can you believe that? I do own a Colorado driver's license last time I checked."

Gregory chuckled. "Just make sure you don't run over any of these old-timers. I heard some like to drag race in their wheelchairs around this hour."

Martin let out a hearty laugh as he sat down behind the wheel. "That's a good one. I only need the car for a couple minutes.

I'll be right back."

"Suit yourself, Commander, I'll be here."

Martin closed the door and whipped out his cell phone to immediately call Commander Blair. He answered after two rings.

"Let's do it," Martin said.

"Everything is in place?"

"I've triple-checked, it's just a matter of Duane being in the house once I get there."

"I don't see why he wouldn't be—he's actually out there to take care of his mother. We pulled some more records and found out that she's suffering from late-stage cancer. She doesn't have much time to live."

Hearing this struck a particular nerve within Martin. He, too, had been caring for his mother, even went as far as risking his life to get her medicine from the year 2064. But while he was gone on that mission, Chris decided to swoop in and slaughter Marilyn like a useless farm animal.

The tinge of guilt didn't last long. Duane would have known Martin's mother was sick and didn't stand up to Chris about his actions. Now Duane would have to suffer the same torment of helplessness that Martin had, an unfortunate bonus in his eyes.

"That's too bad," Martin said. "I'll be sure to leave the mother alone—I'm not a monster, like some people. I'll go in, grab Duane, and be on my way. Will call you when I'm ready."

"Sounds like a plan. Remember, emergency plan in case I don't hear from you in one hour, I'll unfreeze time."

"This should take ten minutes. The GPS says I'm only five from his house."

"Perfect. I'm going to disconnect the call so I can focus and freeze time. Give me about fifteen seconds."

"Thanks, Commander."

Martin hung up the phone and rolled down his window where the driver waited. "Excuse me, Gregory, can you do me a quick favor?"

"Anything, Commander." The kid's eyes bulged at the prospect of doing a personal favor for the commander.

"Can you start clapping your hands for me?"

Gregory put his hands together, an eyebrow raised.

"Just clap like you're watching a sports game. Who do you guys like down here? The Dolphins?"

"Nobody likes the Dolphins, Commander. A lot of golf is watched in this town, but personally I try to get to a Heat game on occasion."

"Well, pretend you just watched Jimmy Butler sink a game-winning shot in the Finals. Start clapping like that."

The driver raised his hands in front of his chest and separated them, a puzzled smirk on his face. His hands never clapped, but remained frozen apart, eyes staring blankly at Martin.

"That's all I needed, thank you," Martin said, Gregory still not moving. He drove off, the GPS frozen, but he had already studied the route during the flight.

He whistled as he turned out of the hangar and onto the road, the street lamps splashing their soft yellow glow on the smooth pavement below. There wasn't another car in sight.

The drive was just over a mile to the final destination, and even with no chance of a car accident, Martin drove the speed limit, reciting the directions in his head as he made left turns and right turns, then a quick dash down a main road before he entered the neighborhood of Hideaway Hills.

It definitely had the appearance of a Florida retirement

141

community. All of the lawns were green and perfectly mani-cured, and American flags hung from the front porch of nearly every house. Porch lights were left on to intimidate potential intruders, and nearly each home had a couple of rocking chairs or swinging benches out front.

Daytime would likely reveal a community of elderly neigh-bors keeping each other company, stopping at each other's houses as part of their morning strolls through the neigh-borhood, sharing updates about their grandchildren back in whatever cold state they had abandoned. Life was simple and innocent, and Martin intended to keep it that way.

Surely they might speculate on where Duane had gone in the middle of the night, but a story like that wasn't exactly drama compared to one of the residents finally receiving their call to the big man upstairs. Perhaps Martin would even do the right thing and let Duane call one of his mother's neighbors to let them know an emergency arose at home and he needed to leave. It wasn't fair to his mother to wake up without her son and no explanation.

A tear ran down Martin's cheek as he thought of his own mother, napping innocently at home when Chris and his chums barged in to take her life. He only hoped she had felt no pain.

Martin turned onto Dutchess Park Road, and his heart immediately started drumming in his chest. He didn't know why he was so nervous. Perhaps because it was his first time out on his own since becoming Commander. Hell, since the campaign, for that matter. He had a team with him everywhere he went during his travels around the continent, happy to have left them behind at the jet for this journey.

The houses on this block appeared to be little ranch-style homes, all piled on top of each other, not more than ten feet separating the properties. He pulled up to the Betts residence and killed the engine, rolling down the window to ensure that time was indeed still frozen. No crickets chirped; no distant white noise of traffic emanated from the main road.

Coast is clear, he thought as he craned his neck for a view through the front window. There appeared to be a dim glow of a TV, but he'd need to get closer to confirm. He stepped out of the car and closed the door quietly, the silence thick.

He patted the pistol in his waistband and started up the path to the front door, plastic flamingos standing out in their flamboyant pink under the night sky. *Who the hell would actually decorate their lawn with this shit?* he wondered, shaking his head in disappointment. He'd be doing Duane the favor of never having to see those horrendous fake birds again.

He reached the front door, the porch light making him feel spotlighted like a prisoner attempting to escape a maximum security facility. The door had windows at the top that Martin could see through by standing on his tiptoes.

The glow had indeed been a TV, the screen frozen on baseball highlights. A hand holding a remote lay on the armrest of a cushioned armchair, but Martin couldn't make out if it was Duane or his mother.

He tried the doorknob to find it locked. *Worth a try.*

Gerald had prepared him for this, sending him with a lock pick to enter the house without leaving any trail behind. Martin pulled the pick out of his pocket, the size of a small screwdriver with a metal tip shaped like the batarangs that Batman throws at his enemies. "It's one of the simplest tools you can use," Gerald had explained, demonstrating on his own office door.

He inserted the pick and drew a deep breath. It was not a matter of jiggling madly until the door magically unlocked.

It required concentration, and he was grateful for the silent night to assist him. He felt around for the pins within the lock, starting at the furthest one back and rotating toward the front until all were pressed upward. Five pins were inside from his count and he had them all moved out of place within a minute, turning his wrist for the final blow that slapped the bolt out of position.

He tried the knob again, and this time it gave, the door creaking open, the sound making Martin paranoid to the point of looking over his shoulder to make sure there wasn't some elderly person just discovering for the first time their ability to resist frozen time.

The odor of bitter cigars immediately rushed Martin's nose, not the most sanitary decision for someone living with his cancer-ridden mother. Unless she was the one smoking, refusing to give up the act until her dying day. Martin had an older uncle who smoked cigarettes while lugging his oxygen tank behind him, the thought now making him want to laugh.

Just get Duane and get the hell out of here. And stop worrying, you are literally alone in this city. No one is here to even see what you're doing.

Ready to ride the brief wave of confidence, Martin stepped all the way into the living room, finding Duane in the recliner, his gaze unmoved from the TV screen. Martin needed everything to look legit and turned off the TV, letting the room fall into darkness, only receiving a slight illumination from the porch light spilling through the front door.

"Let's get you out of here."

Duane wasn't as big as he expected. He had seen pictures and thought of Chris's right-hand man as much beefier than the man sitting in the recliner. He could have let himself go after coming to Florida, falling into the slow-paced lifestyle and all-you-can-eat buffets that surrounded him on a daily basis.

Martin tugged at Duane's left arm and met a bit of resistance, as if the bones were frozen in place, but it eventually gave way and loosened. He hadn't done much exercise since becoming the commander, often forced at the end of long days to decide if he wanted to catch a couple hours of sleep, or spend time in the gym. Sleep always won.

He still watched his diet and didn't lose too much of the strength he had gained from his extensive bootcamp last year. He crouched to Duane's level, accidentally kicking aside an empty beer can on the floor, the aluminum clanging into a wall and creating chaotic sound that almost made Martin gasp.

"Son of a bitch," he muttered under his breath.

He regained his focus and slipped his arms around Duane's sides, hugging him around the waist and clenching his fingers behind his back. Martin's thighs flexed as he tugged and pulled Duane upward, a slight grunt slipping from his lips as he hoisted with all of his energy. "Motherfucker!"

Martin thought his legs might give out and send them both sprawling to the floor, but it never happened. He elevated Duane in his embrace just a few inches above the recliner, but Martin dug into his well of mental strength, willing the body upward and over his shoulder, holding him like a large child needing to be carried to bed after passing out on the living room couch.

He let out a relieved sigh, his arms wrapped around the legs as Duane's arms dangled over Martin's back. "I got you, big boy, and next time, we're going straight for the piggyback method."

Martin knew he'd have to carry Duane up those stairs to get on the jet, but quickly brushed the thought aside, needing to focus on the present. "Say goodbye, because you're either going to end up dead or on one of our famous islands."

He started for the front door, sure to close it behind him quietly with his one free arm. The front lawns were tiny, Martin grateful for the short walk to the car. He reached the passenger side and pulled open the rear door, crouching once more to lower Duane into the vehicle.

This time his legs did give out, but the backseat caught them both. Duane splayed out on his back as Martin fell forward, catching himself on the floor of the car with one exhausted arm. He ran around to the other side to pull Duane all the way through, an action that sent goosebumps up his spine as he remembered doing the same thing with Gerald in 2064 after their companion, Brigham, had been killed in their apartment while they were out in the city.

With Duane securely in the car, Martin panted for his breath as he returned to the driver's seat, firing up the engine and skidding out of the neighborhood like he was being chased by the police.

Once the adrenaline wore off, Martin shouted excitedly. "Wooo! That's how you do it! That's how you win a fucking war!"

It was only one step, but a big one that would certainly send Chris into a frenzy. He backtracked his route, driving much faster as urgency crept into his mind. The clocks were frozen, but he calculated roughly fifteen minutes for his venture into the house and loading Duane into the car. If all went well, he'd be back on the jet with plenty of time to spare and make the call across the ocean for Blair to unfreeze time.

Why haven't we been doing this from the beginning? Why is everyone so afraid of using this ability? Strike didn't want me to use it without proper testing first. They brushed it aside. I could have rescued her this way—but no one wanted to listen.

Martin vowed to never be close-minded to anyone's suggestions during his term as commander. Nearly every Road Runner was brilliant in their own way, and there was never a lack of good ideas. When he had first joined, they were known for having the highest standards of excellence. Everyone he had met was kind and hard-working, ambitious almost to a fault, so consumed by advancing the betterment of the organization.

"Where did that go?" he asked the rear-view mirror where a frozen Duane held his gaze that had been watching baseball on TV. "Did you bastards take it from us? Or did it just fizzle?"

Martin supposed it was a combination of the two factors, and it certainly didn't help having the organization's highest ranking court scurry into hiding like frightened mice.

Chris got to us. He escalated matters to the point where no one wanted to participate in life, let alone the Road Runners.

"Never again. I don't give a shit if it's a Revolter or a Liberator. They will never terrorize us again."

Martin pulled into the hangar, the jet waiting, motivation replacing the paranoia that had clung to him since he arrived in Florida. He pulled the car next to the mobile stairs where Gregory still stood with his hands inches apart, about to clap.

"Let's go, Mr. Betts," Martin said as he killed the engine and let himself out. His newfound ambition sparked a fresh wave of energy and strength. The climb up the stairs seemed less daunting, especially now that he would start with Duane over his back like a younger sibling taking a piggyback ride on their big brother's shoulders.

147

Duane's entire body had finally loosened, making it easier for Martin to maneuver his limbs and prop him into the needed position. The night remained still as Martin climbed the steps, the real possibility of ending this war throbbing like a migraine in his head. Part one was complete, and later this morning the fireworks would begin in Alaska.

20

Chapter 20

As the commander, Martin enjoyed the customization of the jet to his liking. Strike had installed a small corner designated for meditation and yoga. Martin replaced it with a fully-stocked bar and flat screen TVs. Strike had a pantry full of organic and vegan options. Martin ripped that shit out and installed an industrial refrigerator to store the finest meats money could buy.

Martin kept the furniture, however, not caring enough to replace the dark red lounge chairs and matching sofa. He didn't have a decorative bone in his body and wouldn't even know where to begin with that sort of project.

Duane lay on the couch, a limp blob of flesh as Martin raced back down to the car to drop a hundred dollar bill on the driver's seat as a thank-you to Gregory. He dashed back up the steps and closed the aircraft's door.

His pilot sat in the cockpit, frozen with an open paperback held in his lap. Martin scampered around to make sure everything was in place, and once calm, dialed Commander Blair.

"How did it go? Did you catch your guy?"

"Yes, it was actually kind of easy."

"That's what I like to hear. I was keeping an eye on you through the tracking software. There wasn't a soul around you in that neighborhood. Glad everything worked out. Are you ready to let the world keep spinning now?"

"Absolutely. We have a very busy twenty-four hours coming up, and this flight may be the only sleep I get for the next couple of days."

"You got it. Let me know when you need my help again."

"You'll be hearing from me soon. Thank you, Commander."

"Good luck today. We'll be following closely."

They hung up and Martin sat back in his lounge chair, pulling out his pistol and pointing it at Duane. After a few seconds, the jet rumbled as the hum of its engines rose back to life, sending the most subtle vibrations up his back.

A certain tension that lingered in the air while time was frozen vanished, and Martin watched as Duane flailed his arms and sat up.

"What the hell?!" he gasped, his stare bouncing around the jet like a confused bird.

"Welcome," Martin said with a smirk.

Duane jumped off the couch, but didn't make a move toward Martin.

"I suggest you sit down. It's a long flight back to Denver."

"Martin Briar? What are you doing here?"

Martin laughed. "Been out of the loop for a bit, haven't you? Does Chris not keep you updated while you're gone?"

"I asked him to leave me alone while I cared for my mother. Where is she? What did you do to her?!"

Martin raised a steady hand. "Relax. I'm not like you

150

demented pieces of shit. Nothing happened to your mother. She's still sound asleep in her house. I'll let you call one of her neighbors later this morning to let them know you had to leave."

"You had no right! How dare you! That is a dying woman you left abandoned."

"And you had the right to barge into *my* house and kill *my* mother? Don't give me your sob story."

"I wasn't there. I had no involvement."

"Good for you. But I'm sure you knew about it. And what did you do, turn a blind eye? I didn't take you tonight for some sort of revenge, although it is good karma for you to have to experience this. We wanted you for the simple reason of having you in our possession. See, that mansion is going to be bombed today and Chris will be on the run, surely looking for you."

"You'll never penetrate the outer shield—that's impossible," Duane said, pompous.

"Wow, you really don't have a clue what's going on. Good for Chris for not bothering you during your difficult time, but I thought for sure he'd at least keep you up-to-date. Let's see, where to start? First off, I'm the new commander of the Road Runners."

Duane's eyes bulged at the words.

"Secondly," Martin continued. "The shield around the mansion is down. Chris blew up our Alaskan headquarters. Sent a suicide bomber right into the place and *POOF!* Just like that. Then he brought down our hotel on the Las Vegas Strip. Killed thousands of our people and civilians as well. Your boy is on fire, I'll give him that. He's clearly feeling cocky, too, because after our Alaskan office went up, he dropped the shield. It's probably not the dumbest move, seeing as there is no longer a consistent threat there, but why not just keep them up?"

"Oh my God, Chris, no you didn't," Duane said to himself, slapping a hand on his forehead.

"Tell me, Duane... you're really the brains behind Chris. He's just a wild dog trying to ruin people's lives, but you're the one who brings structure to the Revolution, are you not?"

Duane crossed his arms and slowly nodded. "I'm not one to brag about myself, but yes, it's true. Chris is nothing but a sociopath. And he *is* smart when it comes to big picture tasks like plotting major attacks, but the guy has no common sense. I think his invincibility makes him completely reckless. He only worries about himself, and since he can't die, he doesn't have anything to actually worry about."

"I get the sense that you were once a good man," Martin said, not moving the pistol. "It's a shame you had to dirty your soul with the Revolution."

"'Dirty my soul'? *You're* the one who ran away like a coward. You betrayed the Revolution. Chris was ready to bring you into the inner circle. This could very well be you on this couch right now."

"Looks like I made the right decision, then." Martin shot a smirk across the way. "You people are nothing more than a terrorist organization. You should have seen the damage you did in Las Vegas. Zero regard for the innocent lives lost that had nothing to do with this war."

"I don't know what you want from me. I've been in Florida for the last two months—I didn't even know these things were happening."

"I want nothing from you. You don't owe me an explanation. I have what I want by you being on this jet with me. We're not going to hurt you—or your mother. You'll be living in one of our holding cells as long as needed. We'll keep you fed and give you a comfortable place to sleep."

"Then what is this really about? Because at the end of the day, Chris doesn't give a shit. If you told him that you had me as prisoner, he'd probably just laugh and tell you to kill me. This is a man who killed his own wife and shunned his only child to get where he is today. I'm nothing compared to those two."

"Good to know, but it has nothing to do with that. We know Chris is afraid. We've been sparring with words since I came into my position a couple weeks ago. I haven't backed down or cowered to his commands like others. Perhaps I'm making the same mistake as him in thinking I'm invincible."

"But you're not."

"I know that, but I have nothing to live for, so there's not really much of a difference, in my opinion. See, I didn't want this job—they forced me to run in the election and I humored them by agreeing to it. Somehow I ended up winning, and I still don't understand how. I'm never getting my daughter back, you people killed my mother, and Sonya is likely gone forever. So I might as well try to do the right thing by destroying the Revolution. If I die in the process, then I get what I've been afraid to do myself for the past two decades. It's a win-win for me."

"You know, your Road Runners aren't as innocent as you think. They may not physically harm people as often as we do, but they play the mental game. I think everything you told me is the exact reason they asked you to run for the commandership. They study people's lives extensively. They probably know things about your life that you've personally forgotten. A man with nothing to lose is the perfect candidate to make a move on Chris. That way if you die, it doesn't look like an intentional sacrifice—but it is. I've never encountered a more deliberate group of people than the Road Runners. Every single decision is made with a purpose."

"We're just forward thinking and prepared for everything. We have to be when dealing with terrorists like you on a daily basis."

But now Martin wondered. Was he really a pawn in some sort of plot being run from the European Road Runners? Was someone else pulling the levers from across the ocean? He couldn't show any doubt, and instead shouted for his pilot. "We need to get back to Denver – is the jet ready?"

The pilot emerged from the cockpit, eyes studying Duane and the pistol pointed at him. "We're ready, Commander."

"Perfect, let's go!"

The pilot nodded and disappeared to prepare for takeoff.

"You know, Duane, I think we could have worked very well together, whether it was in the Revolution or the Road Runners. I suppose we'll never know, but I feel like we complement each other quite nicely, don't you think?"

Duane stared at Martin with no response.

"You don't need to be so serious," Martin said. "Lighten up—this isn't the end of the world. If we can actually kill Chris, I don't see why we wouldn't let you go."

"You still haven't told me what you need me for."

"My apologies," Martin said with a grin. "We think Chris might seek someone else to inject his blood into to keep his invincibility. We're just picking off people we know he trusts. We'd appreciate your help in naming any other people you might know."

"Fuck you," Duane said sharply, not moving a muscle.

"That's the spirit. Put these on." Martin reached into a bag on the floor and tossed a pair of handcuffs to Duane. "Cuff one to your wrist and the other to the foot rail at the bar."

He nodded toward the bar where Duane looked and saw the shiny golden rail drilled into the floor.

"Are you shitting me? I have to lay on the ground?"

"It's either that or I have to cuff your wrists and ankles together so you can't move. I just want to take a nap. You decide." Martin cocked the pistol, the threatening click lost in the sound of the rumbling jet that started down the runway. "It's a three-hour flight. You can get some sleep, too. Didn't seem like you had gone to bed yet for the night anyway."

Duane shook his head as he rose from the couch and shuffled to the bar, kneeling on the floor as he closed one cuff around his wrist and the other on the rail.

"Tug to show me it's tight."

Duane obeyed and yanked his arm away, the metal clanging as his balled fist stopped a few inches from the rail.

"Perfect, that's all I needed to see. Have a good flight. I'll see you in Denver."

Martin reclined in his lounge chair and let himself drift off to sleep. His brain was exhausted and had no issue dozing, even with all the commotion behind him. The world was ready for the change coming in the morning, and he needed to be, too.

21

Chapter 21

In Barrow, Alaska, away from the drama of a treasonous Councilwoman and middle-of-the-night kidnapping of Duane Betts, a team of Road Runners put on the final touches of their two-week project. They worked at all hours so that progress was constant. They knew what they were working toward, and nobody griped about the long hours, proud to be an integral part of the organization's constantly changing history.

Andrew Wilson, the man tasked with leading the charge in Alaska, examined the placement of the explosive devices from the tunnel they had spent the last two weeks digging. The mansion had retaining walls deeply embedded in the ground, and they were able to find them quite easily. It was the digging around the actual mansion that proved more challenging than anticipated.

Nevertheless, they pushed through. Andrew headed the development team for the Road Runners. Their primary focus was building safe office spaces around the country, maintenance of said properties, and constructing anything the commander might need. His same crew had also built the now-extinct Desert Oasis Hotel in Las Vegas, and hearing of its destruction made everyone want to work even harder on their new tunnel project. Many even took the liberty of signing their names on the concrete retaining walls, the ultimate 'fuck you' to Chris.

Andrew often touted his team as the smartest in all of the Road Runners. They consisted of architects and engineers from every field of practice, and also doubled as a construction crew to create their visions first-hand. They had plenty of experience working underground, considering most Road Runner offices were in a basement, but they had never done so under the cloud of fear that lingered over them every day. They set up camp a quarter-mile from the mansion, across the only road, separated by a wide span of trees that kept them concealed from the mansion's view.

This didn't mean they felt safe, however. They were dealing with the most dangerous man in the world, as far as they were concerned. And if he had happened to go out for a jog through the woods and find their little campground setup, what might he have done on the spot?

But no one ever discovered them. Only the first day of construction had been loud as they dug the initial hole in the ground to begin the tunnel, but by day two they were fully hidden beneath the earth. Digging a quarter-mile tunnel was no small feat, especially on the strict time restraints provided by Commander Briar. But with a crew and a surprising influx of volunteers who simply wanted to come dig as instructed, Andrew was able to create a schedule to meet the seemingly impossible deadline. It was incredible to see how a little bit of determination to end the war propelled people to uncanny levels of focus on the task at hand.

Andrew had examined the bombs, testing their radio signal with one of the volunteers at the campground. All were properly planted, four on each retaining wall all the way around the house. Even without the bazooka, the mansion would surely crumble into itself and cause plenty of harm and death to those inside.

Everything was cleared, only requiring the final word from Commander Briar on the detonation of the bombs and firing the missile. They had also sent a soldier to Barrow to deliver and handle the bazooka. None of the constriction crew had any experience using one and didn't want to botch the critical step.

A ten-minute walk separated the base of the mansion from the campground, and once he stepped out of the tunnel, Andrew promptly lit a cigarette and pulled out his cell phone to call Gerald. It was 7 A.M. in Barrow, the sun not quite breaking the horizon yet.

"Good morning, Mr. Wilson," Gerald greeted.

"Good morning, sir. I just did a final check. Everything is in position and ready, including the bazooka."

"Great. I spoke with our soldier this morning and he knows the position he needs to be in. He will be the closest to the mansion, but still a quarter-mile away."

"That should be fine, our explosions shouldn't create any outward shrapnel."

"Understood. I will have Commander Briar give you a direct call in a couple minutes to authorize the strikes. And Mr. Wilson... thank you. You've led such a flawless project—I can't imagine having anyone else on the job."

"Thank you, sir."

They hung up and the air grew still. Roughly twenty tents were set up within the hundred yard radius of clearing they had discovered, and each one's lamp illuminated in the chilly morning. Everyone had worked tirelessly on the project and wanted to join the festivities in viewing the encore. Many started to emerge from their tents, rubbing their eyes and clutching steaming cups of coffee that had been boiled over a communal campfire.

Soon, the ground would rumble and smoke would rise in the distance. They had a strict exit plan to follow. Surely no one would venture their direction, all focus on the destroyed mansion. Chris would be on the run, and everyone was ready with their own firearms to defend the campground should he happen to stumble their way. Andrew had suggested they disable Chris's jet in the Barrow hangar, but it was too heavily guarded.

Chris had an exit from the scene if he could think fast enough. If not, they just might get the opportunity to capture him today.

Andrew remained skeptical at such a prospect, and only hoped they'd be able to pack up their campsite tonight and head to the hangar where their own jet would be waiting to take them all to Denver where Commander Briar had a celebratory breakfast planned for them the next morning.

His cell phone rang and he looked down to a blocked number. "Hello?"

Those in the campground gathered around in anticipation.

"Hello, Mr. Wilson, this is Commander Briar. How are you and your team doing this morning?"

"We're great. And we are ready."

"Love to hear it. Gerald let me know everything is in place. We're watching from the live stream. We equipped our soldier with a body camera to capture the event. He's already in position and waiting for the green light. I have him on the other line. As soon as you hear the explosion, please detonate the bombs you have planted. Do you have any questions?"

"No, sir. We have been preparing for a long time now. We're ready."

"Very good. Thank you for your hard work, and I look forward to meeting you in person tomorrow morning. You should expect to hear the bazooka in about twenty seconds."

"Thank you, Commander."

The call ended, and the volunteer who was sending the test signals with Andrew came over and handed him the detonator. They nodded to each other, the world falling completely silent as they awaited for the sound that would change their lives.

With the Earth so quiet, Andrew could hear it crying out for an end to the evilness that plagued it every day. An end to the madness and chaos that consumed humanity.

They huddled in a circle, everyone now out of their tents and waiting anxiously. Andrew heard the bazooka fire, a distant *boom!* followed by a wicked *crack!*

He wasted no time in holding the button down on the detonator, trying to press it right through the device. The bombs ran on a five-second delay, so he closed his eyes and waited.

The ground trembled like a light earthquake, the sounds of their bombs drowned out thanks to being underground, but they *felt* it, and that was all they needed to know they had successfully gone off.

"Ladies and gentlemen, we did it," Andrew said. The group howled and cheered in excitement, hugging each other, an invisible burden finally off their shoulders. Commander Briar might go down in history as the man who finally stopped Chris Speidel, but this crew knew their contributions were what made it all possible.

"Everyone relax. We still have protocol to follow. I'm going to check on our soldier and make sure he's okay. Everyone stay armed and ready. We don't know which way Chris will be running."

Andrew tamed their joy, but for good reason. The hard part was done for them, but relaxing could cost them their lives. They were dealing with a madman, after all.

He left his group behind, the weight of satisfaction heavy in the air. The soldier was positioned exactly halfway between the campground and the mansion, having found a spot on the edge of the woods facing the house. It was normally a five-minute walk, but Andrew ran, not so much out of worry, but a nagging curiosity to see the damage done.

He had witnessed numerous attempted assassinations of Chris, each one failing as miserably as the one before. And while this attack was far from a direct assassination, it represented what the entire membership of the Road Runners wanted to see: a suffering Chris, his mansion a pile of smoldering rubble. He arrived to the soldier within three minutes and found him crouched behind a tree trunk, neck craned to watch the faltering mansion. Andrew joined him, fighting for his own view.

What was once a pristine property with its white walls, fake shrubbery, and layered brick paths, now split down the center, the two halves crumpling inward as the final remains of the structure collapsed.

"Oh my God," Andrew whispered, his eyes bulging as a hand moved up to cover his mouth. Every Road Runner on the planet knew what Chris's mansion looked like, perhaps as recognizable as the White House in D.C. for those in the time travel world. But seeing it like this was simply beyond comprehension.

"It's beautiful, isn't it?" the soldier, a scruffy man named Ethan Daniels, asked over his shoulder, a proud grin stuck on his face. "The missile landed dead center. The house was already split before you set the bombs off."

Aside from the smoldering house, Andrew noticed that their bombs had indeed worked. What he had first thought was the mansion's main level was actually the second. The main level was gone, sunk into the ground and collapsed into the basement.

One figure managed to climb out of the rubble, clearly one of the goons who lived inside. He stumbled away from the building where a fire started to grow bigger by the second on the left-hand side of the mansion. He paused, seeming to study the building, before twirling in a circle and falling face down into the dirt.

"Where's Chris?" Andrew asked.

The soldier shrugged. "I haven't seen him."

For a brief moment Andrew wondered if Chris was even inside. They had no way of actually knowing for sure. But that still wasn't the point. Even if he happened to be elsewhere, he'd still have nowhere to return to.

The sides of the house wavered, swaying like tall trees in the wind. The interior had completely collapsed, all the windows and the beautiful, spiral staircase now crumbled into a pile.

More vibrations rumbled the ground, both Andrew and Ethan looking around in confusion.

"Did one of the bombs not go off?" Ethan asked.

"Not to my knowledge," Andrew replied, but the truth was he had no way of knowing for sure. It was possible that one of the twelve bombs didn't go off, but they had visual evidence that the underground attack worked, the mansion a sinking ship.

The vibrations grew louder, bringing with them a strong gust of wind as a dark shadow passed overhead. They looked up to see a helicopter, the deafening white noise of the chopper eliminating their ability to hear anything. Ethan shouted something to Andrew, but he had no chance of hearing it.

The helicopter descended, and Andrew saw three Revolution soldiers hanging out of the sides, long rifles clutched in their grip, surely cocked and ready to fire at any imminent threats.

Once it touched down, Chris emerged from the rubble, his frosty hair black with ash and smoke. Andrew's jaw dropped, not in shock that Chris was alive—that much was expected—but by how quickly a helicopter had arrived to take him to safety. It couldn't have been ten minutes since everything collapsed.

And where the fuck *did Chris come from?*

Eyes had been on the property the whole time, yet there was no trace of him until now. It was like he rose from the underground and barreled through the collapsed remains of his house. The thought sent chills up Andrew's back.

They watched as Chris moved calmly, stepping over shattered furniture, smoking pieces of brick, tiptoeing carefully to not trip. He still wore his black suit, and combined with his blackened face, appeared more like a silhouetted figure rising from hell.

Chris never looked around—or looked back, for that matter. He simply boarded the helicopter without a word to the guards waiting for him. No one followed him.

Andrew and Ethan watched as the helicopter immediately

ascended and flew out of sight, leaving the two back in silence in a matter of seconds.

"Did that really just happen?" Ethan asked.

Andrew fell speechless, two weeks of hard work feeling flushed down the drain. He could only hold on to hope that this attack would still lead to something positive in the Road Runners' future.

22

Chapter 22

Martin and Gerald sat in Martin's office, facing the TV on the wall. They decided to bring in Duane for the festivities, keeping him handcuffed to a metal folding chair. Gerald made it very clear that Duane shouldn't try anything cute with the chair, citing an itch to bash a skull into the concrete floor.

Duane had remained silent during the attacks, not showing a single drop of emotion as his gaze to the TV reminded Martin of that same look he had on his face while frozen in time in his mother's living room.

Martin had granted Duane the phone call to one of his mother's neighbors, done so with a gun to his head to ensure he didn't say anything about his whereabouts. The call wrapped up in a few minutes and Duane already seemed more at ease—as much as he could under the circumstances—knowing his mother was being looked after.

Martin could only smile as he watched the destruction of the mansion, thinking back to the time he had spent there, not knowing who to trust in the world, just wanting a way out of the time travel life. *Oh, how far I've come since then.*

His world had been flipped upside down upon his arrival, and looking back, he was grateful for it. Had he been in any different state of mind, he may have been lulled into Chris's tricks and become a part of his upper establishment like Duane had mentioned.

Instead, he sat here with Duane watching the first pillar of the Revolution fall into a pile of dust. Martin had instructed Ethan to stash the camera where the feed could keep rolling long after they had all cleared out. Ever since Chris had taken off on the helicopter, there had yet to be any signs of additional life rising from the rubble.

The missile had caused enough damage to the upper part of the house that it only took an hour for everything to completely be swallowed up in the flames. It was around this time when the local fire department arrived, a dozen yellow coats sifting through the wreckage after blasting the remains with water to kill the last of flickering flames.

"That's quite the beautiful sight, Commander," Gerald said. "I never thought I'd see the day when this happened."

"It is indeed."

"What are your plans for next steps?"

Martin leaned back in his chair and looked to the ceiling. "I'm gonna capture Mario Webster today and bring him here so that Duane has some company. I understand we learned that Mario helps run the Wealth of Time store secretly stashed in northern Nevada."

"Nevada is a quick trip."

"Indeed. That flight to Florida was brutal. Duane, do you know of anyone else we can purge from Chris's life? I'd hate to give him any hope."

Duane shook his head and spoke for the first time since

arriving in Denver. "He's going to kill you. This does not end well for you."

Martin laughed. "Well, which is it? Because on the plane you told me that he didn't care about you and will let you die. Now he's gonna get revenge on me or try to save you? You can't have it both ways."

"Under normal circumstances, yes, he would let me and Mario die. But now that you've attacked him, and there's no mistaking who did it... He doesn't like being toyed with."

"I'm sooo scared," Martin said sarcastically, smirking. "If Chris wants revenge, then he needs to come face me in person. And that's all we want, isn't it?"

Gerald nodded, holding a gaze to the ground.

"We're ready for Chris. We're ready to end this bullshit war. Chris just can't bear the fact that there are people in the world who disagree with him. *Hate* him. Instead of swallowing his pride, he had to lash out and keep killing us. God forbid anyone in the *world* exist who doesn't agree with Chris Speidel on how to properly use the gift of time travel. And you know what the sad part is? He brings good men like you down to his level. You may not do the evil things he does, but you certainly enable him."

"You don't know anything about our story."

"Then why don't you tell me? We have time—you're not going anywhere."

"Go to hell."

"Funny phrase considering Chris is *from* hell. Say what you will about the Road Runners, but we have always stood up to the evil. I'll be damned if I sit by for my two years in this office and pretend what happens in the future is okay. I know you don't see yourselves as bad people, but genocide against the entire population of Road Runners is far from something good people do."

"We're smarter than you," Duane said, his tone soft. "We're *always* a step ahead of you. If you think Chris didn't have plans for something like this happening, then you're absolutely wrong. Do you think he called someone to come pick him up today? No, plans are in place for any situation that arises. So even if you catch us off guard, we already know what our next move is. We never have to make a decision on the spot."

"Well, I'd say I caught *you* off guard. What was your grand plan for being kidnapped by the Road Runners?"

"You played dirty. You know we have a universal agreement regarding the use of freezing time. You and whoever assisted you—probably that British fuck—will receive your justice for these actions."

"Drop the shit, Duane. We all know you're the last people to administer justice—get off your high horse. Chris killed civilians in our hotel—and that's another universal agreement, so I guess we're even now."

"You don't know shit about our laws or way of life. You've barely been in the time travel world for what, two years? If that. Don't act like you know everything, because you don't know shit. You've been brainwashed by these people to think you're someone important. You're just a pawn in their desperate game to save themselves from their demise. There's a reason the genocide works in the future, and it's not because you're all the geniuses you think you are."

"Big words for a guy handcuffed to a chair. Gerald, unless Duane here has anything to offer us in terms of who else he'd like to have as a roommate, please take him back to the holding cell. I don't want to see him until it's time to ship him off to the island."

"Yes, sir."

Gerald stood and uncuffed Duane from the chair, leading him out the room without another word. Gerald returned a minute later, shaking his head. "When did you become so callous?"

"What do you mean?" Martin asked, frowning.

"I mean it as a compliment, don't get me wrong. You were flat out cold-blooded. I've known you as a reserved guy, even after winning the election, but that was impressive. You tore him to shreds, and anything he said to you bounced right off."

"I don't know what you want me to stay. I genuinely hate the Revolution. I've seen what they do to the world and have experienced it myself. I don't need any more motivation than closing my eyes and picturing what they did to my mom. One hundred percent unforgivable. They can all burn in hell, and I'll see to it that they do."

Gerald laughed. "You keep doing your thing. What's the plan for getting this Mario guy?"

"I received confirmation that he's in Nevada, not in any particular city, just in the middle of the desert nowhere near any roads. I'm thinking you and I fly in and take him, no need to freeze time or anything if he's in such a remote location."

"Don't you think Chris will be on his way there?"

"We're keeping an eye to see if arrives there, but I don't think so. It wouldn't be wise for him to go to such a remote place. He needs all of the protection he can get right now. I think he's going to hide out where there is much heavier traffic."

"And no word on Sonya yet?"

Martin shook his head. "I suppose Chris has a better chance at finding her first, but we have people looking. She could be anywhere—she's resourceful. I wouldn't be surprised if she

169

found a way to Europe or Africa to hide. Which, if that's the case, we're wasting our time."

"Nothing is a waste of time if it leads us to Chris. When do you want to leave for Nevada?"

Martin checked his watch, lips pursed as he thought. "Might as well leave now. No point in sitting around. The quicker we can get this done, the quicker we can send a message to Chris."

"I'll call the pilot and have him prepare the jet. Meet me in ten minutes to drive over?"

"That works."

Gerald let himself out of the office, leaving Martin to stare at the wall of past commander portraits, each one with a shit-eating grin on their face.

"You all failed," Martin said to them. "But I won't."

Chapter 23

Duane was right; the Revolution had a plan ready for any possibility that might arise. The fall of the mansion in Barrow was no exception, the house equipped with an alarm system that notified critical personnel in case of an attack. Once the alarm tripped, the private jet's pilot was instructed to get out of Barrow and fly 200 miles east to Prudhoe Bay. A helicopter was stashed five miles south of the mansion where four Revolters lived, their sole purpose to get Chris out of Barrow as quickly as possible should a situation arise. They lived in solidarity, not a single road reaching their home.

When the alarms sounded, they sprang into action, abandoning their house and heading for the collapsed mansion. Within two hours they dropped off Chris in Prudhoe Bay where his jet awaited, and returned to their personal homes in different locations across the country.

As much as he loved it, the mansion wasn't everything. Chris had half a dozen other properties to work out of, not to mention the hundreds of offices around the continent where Revolters gathered every day.

The true pain in the ass, for this particular circumstance, was the need to find an entirely new crew of soldiers to protect the next property. He would need to call Duane back from Florida—and how he'd hate him for doing so—but these were desperate times. He didn't fear the Revolution was in any serious danger, but if swift actions weren't taken, the Road Runners' next attack could prove costly to their stability.

Teams already lived in each of the properties scattered around the continent, mainly to monitor the area for Road Runner activity. After a conference call with each location, Chris chose the small town of Three Creek, Idaho. Located on the southern border of the state, it remained a remote town with no reported population. An hour drive into Twin Falls was all it took to find grocery stores to stock up on supplies for the house.

Chris had become used to the glory of his own privacy in the mansion, but that would quickly end. While he'd still have his own office and bedroom, the house in Three Creek was a ranch-style home with a basement, equipped to shelter a maximum of ten people.

Unlike Barrow, Three Creek did not have its own airport, leaving Chris to fly into Twin Falls and catch a ride south to his new home. Chris wasn't concerned about any of these logistics, however. He had people to make sure everything ran smoothly for his arrival. All he cared about was Sonya, and he phoned Thaddeus, who was leading the mission of finding what exactly happened to his missing daughter.

"Tell me you have an update," Chris said, bemused as he stared out of his jet's window.

"We have everything you need," Thaddeus said, a clear smile visible in his voice. "A gentleman by the name of Steve Scott let Sonya know she needed to run."

"Steve?!" Chris gasped. "*My* Steve? Are you sure?"

"Absolutely. He told her we were coming and helped her out of the Denver apartment immediately. Sonya asked no questions and went along with it."

"Goddammit!" Chris punched the arm rest on his lounge chair.

"Calm down, Chris. We know where she is."

"Already?" he asked, rubbing the side of his hand where he had struck the chair.

"It's not that difficult to track someone down when they are stuck in the same year. We spotted her driving east and followed her to D.C. She's living outside the city in a little ramshackle apartment building. We've had a car parked outside for the last two days, just watching her routine."

"Thank God. Does it look like an easy place to break into?"

"One of the easiest. There's not any sort of security, or even a person who'd give a shit if we went in and pulled her out of the building."

"That's what I like to hear. Can your team stay there for a couple more days?"

"That shouldn't be a problem, but why?"

"Have them stay alert. I have a hunch the Road Runners are trying to find her. No clue if they're close, but if so, they'll send Martin Briar to try and lure her out."

"The new commander? Why would he risk himself like that?"

"Let's just say he's a man who can't help but follow his heart. If he does show up, you have my blessing to wipe out any and all of the crew traveling with him. Then bring him *and* Sonya to me. What a little party that would be."

173

"And if he doesn't show up, when can we plan to take her ourselves?"

"I'd like to do it myself, if you don't mind. If I know my daughter, she'll put up a fight against you, might even kill some of your people. She can try that with me, but she'll get nowhere. Whatever you do, *don't* kill her. We need her alive."

"Understood."

"I need to make another call. I'll reach out tomorrow," Chris said, and ended the call, quickly dialing Duane.

He waited as the phone rang and rang. It never went to voicemail, and after a whole minute of no answer, Chris hung up and tossed his phone aside.

"You're killing me, Duane."

As if answering a prayer, the cell phone rang, showing Duane's name on the caller ID. Chris snapped it up and answered. "Don't you know we're in a time of crisis, Duane? Do you not check your emails?"

"Hello, Chris. How are you doing?" a familiar voice asked.

"Martin? What are you doing with Duane's phone?"

"Didn't Duane tell you? We're best friends now. I made him an offer he couldn't refuse, and now he's a proud Road Runner."

"I call bullshit. Duane would never do that."

"Then why do I have his phone?"

"You kidnapped him, you son of a bitch. Where is he?"

"I've never seen you so angry, simmer down. I've also never seen you with black hair. I understand that vinegar and shampoo will get that soot right out and have you looking good as new."

"Tell me where Duane is—I need him."

"What's the matter, Chris? Afraid you can't keep going

without little ol' Duane? He told us how you treated him like shit, made him do all the dirty planning for your attacks. And then you tried to refuse to let him spend the final days with his dying mother. Duane hopes you burn in hell."

"You cocksucking *LIAR*!" Chris shrieked.

Martin laughed into the phone. "I won't lie, I love seeing you like this."

"I'll have you know that we will find Duane and then remove you from this planet."

"That's big talk for a guy with nowhere to live."

Chris smiled, reeling in his emotions, understanding how his anger might show as weakness to Martin on the other end of the phone. "Marty, my apologies. I'm sure you can appreciate that I'm upset. Is there perhaps something we can negotiate for Duane's release?"

"No."

"I can offer you Sonya."

"You don't have Sonya."

"Ahhh, that is correct, but I do know where she is. And I have a team just waiting for her to step outside."

"Even if that's true, you wouldn't give us Sonya. We'll just kill her. You might as well sign your own death certificate."

"Has being commander changed you that much, Marty? I thought you *loved* Sonya. Why on Earth would you allow her to be killed?"

"I wouldn't, but there are too many people here who would. I can only do so much."

"But you're the leader. Do you not have the respect of your followers?"

"I have more respect than you'd ever know. People fear you, but they don't respect you."

"I suppose that's a fine line, wouldn't you say?"

"I'd say you're a murderous dictator, and I'm someone trying to cleanse the world of you."

Chris howled with laughter. "There he is, I knew the old Martin was still alive in there. It's a shame we had to meet at this particular moment in time. I do believe you and I could have made a great team under different circumstances."

"Tell me where Sonya is. She doesn't deserve to live as a prisoner with you."

"Prisoner? She's my daughter. She'll have a fabulous life without ever having another worry. Certainly won't have to look over her shoulder to make sure you Road Runners aren't hunting her down. Imagine a life of peace for the woman you love."

"Peace doesn't exist with you around. You're a magnet for chaos and death."

Chris giggled like a child. "I'll be sure to put that on my gravestone. I see I'm getting nowhere in this conversation, Marty. Unless you're going to make an offer to release Duane, then we have nothing further to discuss. I need to get back to work on how to send the knockout blow to your pathetic organization."

Chris hung up the phone without giving Martin the chance to respond. Anger boiled within, but he would find Duane and free him. And soon enough he'd have Sonya back by his side, and the world would be right again. The jet started its descent into Twin Falls, and Chris reclined to try and relax before heading to his new home.

24

Chapter 24

Martin had brought Duane's cell phone with him on the plane ride to Nevada, knowing Chris would attempt to reach out to his most trusted confidant. He enjoyed listening to Chris lose his mind at the onset of the call, but the fun ended once Chris grew serious. It was only a matter of time before Chris retaliated, and Martin needed to counter with urgency of his own.

Gerald joined him on the jet, taking a much-needed nap during their ninety-minute flight, but Martin was wide awake, and would have been even if Chris never called. There were too many possibilities brewing in his mind for a nap. He issued a call for more security at the Denver office now that they were hosting a prominent Revolter, hopeful for a second on their return flight home.

If Chris really knew where Sonya was, he'd have to go into 2064 to get her. Martin called for more eyes in that particular year, sending all available agents to keep an eye out for Sonya without entering the big cities and risking their lives.

Two weeks into the role of commander, Martin had cultivated a strong understanding of all the resources available to him. He had sent out a request for numerous reports over the weekend, and some started to trickle into his inbox. The one he most looked forward to was from the Road Runners' historians, outlining their past attacks against the Revolution and how long it typically took for Chris to retaliate. On average it was a week, but Martin wanted to prepare for the worst case scenario of three days, just in case. He believed it might even be a couple of weeks, being that Chris had to adjust to a new lifestyle and find a new circle of soldiers to keep around him.

"Commander Briar," the pilot announced over the plane's PA system. "We have a situation—you may want to come take a look."

The crackled voice through the speakers woke Gerald, slow blinking as he cleared the fog out his head. Martin didn't wait for him and entered the cockpit.

"What's wrong?"

"Our destination has just come into view," the pilot said, raising a finger out the windshield. Martin looked, but had no idea at what. He saw the vast desert, its solid sandy color stretching as far as they could see. "Use these and point them to that small blob."

Martin saw now that it had been pointed out, and grabbed the pair of heavy-duty binoculars the pilot handed over. They were perhaps one hundred miles away, but these binoculars showed a clear view of the Wealth of Time store. The nostalgia of seeing that building made Martin dizzy to the point of swaying off-balance.

Parked outside of the store were six different cars, all of them black.

"Mario is not alone at that store," the pilot said.

"Impossible. We had scouts check out the area last week.

They said three days passed without a single person stopping at the store. There aren't even any roads that lead there—I don't understand."

"Then it has to be Revolters," Gerald said from behind, his massive frame filling the entire doorway to the cockpit. He ducked his head and stepped all the way in. "If no one else can reach it, then they have to be people who know about it. Chris probably called for reinforcements at all of his properties as soon as we blew up the mansion. He has the resources to make that sort of call. I'm actually surprised there's only a few cars there and not a whole army."

"What are we supposed to do?" Martin asked. "Go home?"

"That's the safest bet," Gerald said, scrunching his face. "I can't think of any nearby locations we could pull Road Runners from to help us. The closest is Reno, and that's a three-hour drive."

"These jets don't come with any guns on them?" Martin asked.

"I'm afraid not," the pilot said. "They are built to absorb any potential hits, but that's it. If we were the size of a commercial airliner, we could probably land and I'd just run the building over. But it looks a little too big for this jet to do something like that."

Martin sighed. "Why don't we have an air force?"

Gerald chuckled. "Because the real Air Force would just shoot us down. We already have a hell of a time getting flights approved by air traffic controllers, but we've been able to get some of our own into that department. I've heard in the 90's you'd have to wait six hours or so for clearance to hop in the jet and takeoff. There's a reason we keep our attacks at ground level—nobody's trying to get locked up in the American justice system. That puts all of us at risk if our secret was to leak, and would make things too complicated. We have to fly under radar and be crafty."

"That all makes sense. Goddammit, turn the plane around. I can't believe this is happening."

"That's the right call, Martin," Gerald said. "If it were even a couple people, I'd say let's just show up and kick ass. But that many cars in the lot? There could be up to twenty of them inside. We'd have no chance."

"Unless time was frozen," Martin said with a smirk. "Can we land a bit further away where they couldn't see us?"

"It's an open desert," the pilot said. "We can land anywhere, and I can drive you as close as you'd like to try," he replied without breaking his stare from the windshield.

"We should have just planned it to be safe, but let me call Blair and see if he can help us."

Martin left the cockpit and picked up the phone installed on the jet, one that had direct service to the other commanders and all Lead Runners across the continent. The phone rang four times and Martin grew antsy. It would have been late evening in England, not quite bedtime, not that commanders bothered going to sleep.

He picked up on the seventh ring.

"Commander Blair, it's Martin, how are you?"

"Good. Is everything okay?"

"It can be, with your help. We are flying above northern Nevada right now, had plans to swipe another one of Chris's goons. It's a remote location and all of our intelligence suggested he lived in this place alone. But now that we're close, we see he has some company. Would you be able to freeze time in a few minutes so we can go in and get our guy?"

"Jesus Christ, Martin, this isn't how this works. Research has to be done before we do this, and we like to inform the other Warm Souls that we have contact with, so they know to expect it. I'm not comfortable doing this."

Martin squeezed the phone in his grip, frustrated, but understanding the concerns. "I get it, but we're in a bind here. We bombed the mansion successfully, as I'm sure you've heard. I spoke with Chris earlier—it's not going to be pretty. I don't know what he's planning, but he's going to retaliate in a big way. And if we can't have at least two of his sidekicks, then I'm not sure we have any leverage. We need him to feel alone so we can try to negotiate him out of harming any more Road Runners."

"Dammit, Martin, this is your war. *You* decided to escalate matters to this point. You couldn't have just waited one more day to blow things up, made sure you had all the people you wanted first, then fire off the bombs? *You* fucked up. You made a bad call and now innocent Road Runners will probably pay for it."

"With all due respect, Commander Blair, we have already paid our fair share of dues in this war. I'm glad that things are much more peaceful where you live, but we don't have that luxury. You get our reports, but you just don't understand what it's like here. People live in fear every day. *Everyone* was in hiding during our election. Our own fucking Council went MIA, and five of them still haven't said a damn word to me about their intent to return. Can you even grasp what this would be like? Are you able to pretend for one moment what it would be like for you to manage this for all of Europe?"

"I'm afraid I'll never truly understand," Blair said softly.

"I know. All throughout history, countries have helped

other countries who were taken over by dictators. Chris is no different, it's just within our own population where he's causing the damage. I don't understand why we can't help each other. If our roles were reversed, I wouldn't hesitate to send help your way."

"Our Bylaws were written very specifically. We don't want to get tangled up in world wars like the rest of civilization. Our focus is on peace for our communities."

"Well, fuck the Bylaws. I'm asking you, man to man, to do the right thing—the ethical thing—and help out a struggling people. I'm not even asking you to send over your best soldiers. I just want *you* to freeze time for thirty minutes, and then unfreeze it, so that *we* can put ourselves in better position to get rid of Chris and live the life of peace that you're so proud of."

Sweat had formed around Martin's forehead as his body temperature raised with the boiling rage inside. Silence poured from the phone, and Martin wondered if Blair had hung up during his rant, ready to rip the cords out of the wall if so.

"Sorry, Commander Briar, I can't do it this time," Blair finally said. "Let me know with some advance notice the next time you need my help."

Now Blair hung up, and Martin placed the receiver back on its hook with a wide, deranged grin.

Gerald had stood in the cockpit doorway with his jaw hanging.

"Goddammit, turn the plane around!" Martin cried, returning to the cockpit. "We're not getting any help on this."

"You got it, Commander." The pilot flicked some switches on his panel and asked Martin and Gerald to step outside and buckle up while he navigated toward the opposite direction.

Martin stared out the window the whole time, fuming.

25

Chapter 25

Chris wasted no time in changing his mind about Sonya. He wanted her in his house *tonight.* Once they touched down in Twin Falls, Chris told the pilot to refuel the jet and prepare for a cross-country flight to D.C. He'd be back in a couple of hours for the trip.

Chris sat in the back seat of a town car, livid from his phone call with Martin for the entire hour drive to his new residence in Three Creek. The driver didn't say a single word, surely sensing the palpable rage lingering in the car.

All he needed to do at his new house was greet the crew who had been living there and relieve them of their duties. With the house being smaller, everyone who would stay there had to be carefully chosen. Besides, these particular crews—glorified house sitters—understood the terms of their jobs and that it would end should Chris ever need to move in.

Chris thanked them and checked on the room that served as his office, a lone desk in the corner with a monitor and keyboard visible. The office had two small windows with obstructed views outside, both cut off by a thick piece of shrubbery that needed trimming. One thing Chris hated was an ugly exterior, no matter how remote of a location he lived. He needed his Revolters to know that he was a man of great power, but more importantly he wanted the Road Runners to know they were trying to mess with a king among kings.

A god, Chris reminded himself as he scanned his dismal new office. *You have always been, and always will be a* god.

He had accrued a list of potential soldiers to protect the new home after a phone call to Mario Webster. Security couldn't wait, and a team needed to be assembled and bound for Idaho immediately. Mario assured him that a full squad would be there before sundown. At the time, Chris didn't know he'd be in D.C. during their arrival, but that didn't matter. They could all settle in and get acclimated with each other and the new house.

Disgusted by the downgrade in his lifestyle, Chris left the house and sat for another boring drive back to Twin Falls. "You must want to blast your brains out making this drive over and over," Chris said to the driver, who only responded with a light chuckle and a "Yes, sir."

While downtime was rare for Chris, he'd typically spend it reflecting on his past. He liked to trace back the timeline of events all the way back to when he was just a hard-working father and husband, grinding away at the factories to collect a measly check that kept food on the table. But not this time. All he could picture was Martin Briar's dead body, Chris standing over it with blood dripping from his mouth after having just taken a bite out of his old friend's throat. *Like mother, like son.*

Chris grinned at the thought, and would work to make it a reality after bringing Sonya back home to safety. His violent fantasies helped pass the time on the drive back to the jet, and they had arrived much faster than anticipated. He boarded the plane, where he'd spend the next three hours brewing more dark thoughts about Martin.

* * *

Chris immediately jumped forward to the year 2064 once they landed in D.C. He made the switch and had his driver take him straight to the apartment complex where they had found Sonya. During the tail end of the flight, Chris had managed to push Martin out of his thoughts and focus on the task at hand. He wanted to ensure Sonya's safety for his own sake, but would also be willing to dangle her in front of the Road Runners like bait.

It had been quite a while since he visited the nation's capital, especially this far into the future. Seeing the Capitol building in the distance, having been remodeled with pure gold, put a smirk of satisfaction on his face. The Revolution's work had always been a gradual process, quietly taking over local governments as they worked their way to the big stage.

When President Poe was sworn in, the Revolution held many private parties around the country, knowing they had achieved their ultimate goal of ruling the United States. Canada would be next, followed by Mexico and the rest of central America. Once the Revolution had complete political influence over the entire continent, it would only be a matter of time before they started ruling the rest of the world.

As long as everything continued on the path he had already carved, that beautiful future awaited. And to ensure that, he needed to bring Sonya home where the Road Runners had no chance of killing her.

They drove the half-hour trip from Ronald Reagan to College Park, where the university had been closed down in the early 2040's and moved within the downtown city limits, inside the confines of the electric fence that kept the poor and the Road Runners out. The old college town was nothing more than the new slums that had become widely normal across the country.

They arrived as the sun started to set, an orange glow cast over the brick building with barred windows and graffiti. A Pepsi vending machine flickered next to the main entrance, a band of pigeons standing guard on top.

"Quite the fall from the penthouse," Chris said. "There should be a black van parked around the back of the building."

The driver obliged and pulled around where the van faced away from the apartment complex, parking right next to it. Chris let himself out and rapped a fist on the van's rear doors.

The double doors swung open and revealed the two Liber-ators who had been staking out the property for the last few days.

"Hello, gentlemen," Chris said with a wide grin. "And what are your names?"

"I'm Mark," said the man on the left side of Chris. He had wavy red hair and freckles covering every inch of his body. "And this is Hank."

"Mark and Hank? Those are your real names?"

"Why would we make our names up?" the man named Hank asked, his tired eyes complementing his gray hair.

"Just like to be sure. There's nothing to fear. You boys have done great work, and I owe you. I'll be taking it from here, though."

Disappointment spread across both of their faces.

"Did Thaddeus not tell you?" Chris asked, an eyebrow cocked.

They looked at each other and shrugged. "He mentioned a few days ago that you *might* want to get the girl yourself, but we haven't heard from him since."

Chris shook his head. "I'm sorry that was not properly communicated to you guys. Please understand it's not that I just needed you to do the hard work. My daughter is dangerous and wouldn't hesitate to kill you both on the spot. Not the case with me. She *can't* kill me."

"Understood, sir," Hank said. "Is there anything we can help you with?"

"Just let me know the apartment number she's in and be ready to drive when I come out with her. You boys up for a trip to the airport?" Chris would rather use the van to conceal Sonya.

"Yes, sir," Mark said. "And she's that apartment." He pointed to the second floor, center window. "Number 212."

"Perfect, give me a few minutes and I'll be right out."

Chris marched away as they slammed the van doors shut. He whistled as he entered the building, a strong whiff of ammonia flooding his senses and making his eyes water. The rear entryway had a lobby that housed a wall of small silver mailboxes for the residents. More graffiti covered the boxes, some of them cracked and split open. From the lobby, a hallway ran toward the front entrance, chips in the white walls that had long eroded to a more yellowish color. A few craters were visible in the drywall, perhaps where a fist or skull had landed. An ugly maroon carpet covered the floor, the edges frayed and peeling away from the walls.

It's a good thing we keep these people out of the cities. No wonder our downtowns are so clean now.

Chris stepped out of the lobby and into the hallway, a crooked sign hanging above that directed him to the stairwell. He cracked open the door, expecting a raccoon or rat to dash out, but was surprised to find the stairwell rather tame compared to the rest of the place. A couple of gang tags were scribbled on the walls, but the stairs were otherwise in pretty good shape.

He climbed the steps, still whistling his tune up to the second floor where he pulled open the door to find a similar hallway, only less trashed compared to the main level. He wanted to call out for Sonya, maybe bang on the walls as he walked down the hallway, like Jack Torrance in *The Shining,* until barging into her apartment.

Room 212 was in the middle of the hallway and Chris took soft steps toward the door, chipped and scratched wood that looked as welcoming as the rest of the building. He pressed his ear against it, but heard nothing from inside. The neighbor next door, however, had a screeching TV loud enough for the rest of the floor to hear.

Chris rapped his knuckles on Sonya's door and stepped back. It had no peephole, so his eyes dropped to the sliver of light splashing from underneath the door, waiting to see her shadow. After a few seconds, it never came, and he knocked once more.

"Sonya, darling, open up," he called in a normal tone, not expecting to be heard. He wondered if she had an exit plan for this exact scenario. The only way out, while keeping the door closed, would be through the window two levels high. A jump from that height wouldn't kill her, but would likely shatter her ankles or knees, deeming her useless if her goal was to run away.

189

Unless she has a rope to let herself down, Chris thought. The van out back would certainly catch her, if that was the case.

He knocked again, and this time shouted loud enough to be heard over the obnoxious TV next door. "Sonya, open the door. Daddy's home!"

He stepped back and crossed his arms, shaking his head. She wasn't going to open the door. Her shadow never appeared, and she was probably hiding in the bathtub waiting for him to leave. Her loud neighbor likely made it impossible to make out the voice calling her name from the hallway. Hell, maybe she wore earplugs if this was the norm for a random weekday afternoon, and never heard the knocking.

He reached out and jiggled the doorknob, finding it loose, but very much locked. He looked around the hallway, still not having seen anyone emerge from their glorious fortress, and decided a gunshot in the middle of the day was exactly what this place needed to cap off the ambiance. He rarely carried a gun, seeing as he was never in true danger, but brought his along on this trip just in case he needed to fend off a group of attackers. His guards normally took care of those matters, but they were all buried under his mansion in Alaska—the good ones, at least.

He couldn't recall the last time he had even fired a gun, and smirked at the fact that he was only using it because he didn't have a screwdriver to take down the doorknob. He cocked the pistol and fired a round into the doorknob. It dropped in an instant and opened a hole for Chris to look through.

Rather than peeking and risking a slug in his eyeball (it would be painless, but a hassle), he kicked the door, watching as it ripped a chain lock out of the wall while it swung all the way open.

Sonya stood in the corner of her living room furthest from the door, a shotgun aimed right at Chris.

"Goddammit!" she shrieked. "Why?!"

"Good to see you, too, darling. Can we have a word?"

Chris entered the apartment and closed the busted door behind him.

26

Chapter 26

Once Chris was inside, Sonya tossed her gun back on the kitchen table. *No point in wasting rounds on him,* she thought.

"How did you find me?" she asked, crossing her arms, knowing her whole plan was officially done.

"Angelina, dear, you weren't that hard to track down."

"Don't you *ever* fucking call me that!" Sonya screamed through clenched teeth, spit flying from her lips as her arms trembled.

"Brings back some memories, doesn't it, *Sonya*?" Chris replied with an evil grin. "Like I said, you weren't hard to follow considering you're stuck in this year. And to think being trapped in 2064 seemed like the safest way to continue your life away from those salty Road Runners. But, my God, aren't they *persistent*? To a fault, you could say. I understand you got word that my team was coming to get you?"

Sonya nodded. "You could have called me yourself to tell me, but like always, you hide like a chickenshit behind your drones."

"Drones, dear? Those are human beings, many who helped

me raise you after your mother died."

"Murdered. She didn't die, she was *murdered*. By you."

"We can't dwell on the fine details of the past, *Sonya*. Do you really think your mother would serve any useful purpose in this world today? Can you imagine her staying by my side once I became the Keeper?"

"None of that should matter. You could have let us both live without you. If you wanted to leave, then you should have just done that. No reason to destroy the entire family."

"Look, we can fight about this again, and probably will for the rest of our lives—which will be a long time. But I didn't come here for that."

"No shit, Sherlock. You're here to finish the job your sorry-ass robots couldn't and bring me home to hold in prison."

"I would *never* hold you prisoner. You're my daughter. My beautiful, strong-willed daughter."

"If I'm not your prisoner, then leave. Let me be."

Chris looked around the apartment. "Leave you in *this* place? Even if everything was fine in the world, I wouldn't let you do that."

"Beats living in your golden palace and pretending that life is fun. You know money and glory don't mean a damn thing to me. You pretend like giving me shopping sprees and dinners out with a nearby table full of guards is fun. It's a bullshit way to live. I haven't once felt in danger in this place, and it's swarming with Road Runners."

"Yes, but not the productive ones—they're the ones still after you. Need I remind you that the most powerful Road Runner right now is still very much infatuated with you?"

"Martin doesn't know what he wants. Our relationship has always been a delusion to him, and that still hasn't changed.

193

He's a good guy, and that's why I'm staying out of his way—for his own protection."

"How sweet of you, caring for people who would kill you in a heartbeat if they only had the chance. It just so happens, though, that Martin's safety is not what I care about. I guess you could say I'm more interested in taking an up close look at his guts and arteries."

Chris grinned as he waited for a reaction from Sonya that never came. She was certainly no newcomer to his mind games, and a reaction was all he sought half the time. For Chris, a reaction revealed weakness in a person, an opening to attack whatever sensitivities might lie within. Once he discovered it, he became a shark unable to help himself as he pounced all over a single drop of blood in the water.

Sonya was years beyond falling for his bullshit. "Where are we going?" she asked, ignoring his last statement about Martin's guts.

"Have you ever been to Idaho?"

"Can't say I have. Why not Alaska?"

"My mansion is gone. You friend, Martin, bombed it to pieces."

Sonya shook her head. "So this is all about getting revenge. When will you stop?"

"My home is gone, why wouldn't I get revenge?"

"Because it will never end. I'm sure you deserved this. You've done plenty in your past to warrant people wanting to drop bombs on your house. Let me guess, though, you're innocent, right?"

Chris smirked. "I ruffle some feathers, sure."

"And you've never bombed anyone, or wiped out a room full of Road Runners just because you were having a bad day?

You seem to forget that I worked very high up with the Road Runners—I know all of the dirty shit you've done. You should be grateful it's just your obscene mansion that was ruined."

"Well, everyone who lived with me died, too."

"Duane's dead?!" Sonya gasped. He was the closest thing to family that Sonya had during her childhood and adolescent years. Duane was more of a father figure than Chris, in fact, always happy to listen to her concerns and ask how school was going—things Chris lacked the emotional intelligence to do.

"Duane is fine. He was in Florida with his mother, but now Martin has him held hostage."

"What the hell has been going on since I left?!" Sonya asked, her face scrunched in confusion. "It's only been a few days and everything has changed."

"It has, and that's why it's important you come with me. We need to be together for more than just keeping me alive. I need you to convince Martin to release Duane. I know the Road Runners want you dead, but Martin calls the shots. He won't plan any more attacks on me if he sees even one glimpse of you by my side. He won't risk it because of his delusion."

"You want me as bait," Sonya said flatly. "You're not afraid of attacks—they do nothing to you. You want to lure Martin."

"As much as I'd like to think that would work, I have no way of knowing how Martin will act aside from ceasing any fire in my direction. Sure, nothing he does will kill me, but I can't keep moving from location to location. I'm already sick of the Idaho house and I was only there for five minutes. It's a miserable shack." He looked around the apartment once more. "But it *is* better than this place."

"You can stop—I know this place is awful. I was only here to be safe from you."

Chris grinned, revealing nearly all of his teeth. "Sonya, I will provide you with safety. I need you to work with me and play a little charades for Martin. We all know how phenomenal of an actress you are, and if you can do one last performance, I'll refill your bottle of Juice."

This grabbed her attention as she locked her gaze onto Chris. "Show me the Juice and let me test it to make sure it works—you can come with me to be safe. And I'll do it."

She had every intent on running as far from Chris once this was all over, but clearly a lack of Juice made hiding impossible. If she could jump to a different era each week—maybe even everyday—it made the task of hunting her down that much more difficult, although never impossible with the amount of manpower Chris had around the globe and all throughout time.

"What exactly are you going to make me do?" she asked, still not breaking her death glare toward her estranged father.

"I'm still trying to figure that out, but we'll definitely hijack the Road Runners' TV stream and make an appearance together. May just have you act like a damsel in distress for theatrics."

When have theatrics ever worked well for you? she thought.

"If we can lure Martin away to meet us on his own—with Duane—then this will all have been worth it. I'll let you go."

"So this is going to be the first time you lie, huh? Now that your back's on the wall, you're no longer a man of your word?"

"On the contrary, dear, I'll be keeping my word. I said you will be released in exchange for Duane. I never said anything about Martin's fate in between that little transaction."

"You know he won't be alone. And if you kill him, they'll have no one to stop them from killing me."

"No one's killing you as long as I'm around," Chris said with a grin, not reassuring Sonya one bit.

"No one will kill me as long as I have new Juice. Not you, not them. You'll never find me again."

"Oh, Sonya, dear, don't you know I'll always find you? My blood flows in your veins. We're connected forever, and I'll chase you to the end of time."

She glared at him while she bit her bottom lip to keep from speaking. He was busting out all the guns to earn a reaction from her. *I'll chase you to the end of time*, she repeated in her head. That was the same line Chris often told Sonya's mother, back when he was capable of love like a normal human being. Back when Sonya believed her parents would be together forever, caring for each other into old age. Before time travel, Revolters, or Road Runners. A simple time when they were a happy family. They may have had their challenges, but they had each other. And that bond between a family could face any obstacles thrown their way.

She reflected on this particular line, and wondered just how much it foreshadowed her father's life. *To the end of time. Was there a part of his subconscious that knew he would see the end of time?* He had spoken this line as far back as Sonya could remember. Every time he said it, he planted a kiss on her mother's forehead, making it such a distinct memory.

She dismissed his words to not let him manipulate her mind by stirring up old memories. *It's my mind, and I control it,* she assured herself.

"Let's just get this over with," she said. "So I can get my Juice and be out of your life."

Chris smirked and waited for Sonya to join him at the door where they'd leave 2064 behind forever.

27

Chapter 27

Over the next seven days, while Chris and Sonya settled into their new home in southern Idaho, Martin and Gerald spent most of their time waiting for the breaking news of an attack on one of their buildings.

But none ever came, and with each passing day they grew a bit more concerned that the attack was surely right around the corner. Chris Speidel simply wouldn't allow his mansion to be bombed without retaliation. He was incapable of turning the other cheek.

A wave of confidence made its way through the entire organization, however. Gone were the calls for a recall vote, replaced by Road Runners crawling out of the shadows and attempting a return to normal life. They were still encouraged to remain vigilant and keep an eye out for those around them. Martin suggested any large gatherings of Road Runners occur only when the invitations were sent out within an hour of the event's start time to prevent the information from slipping into the wrong hands.

With the resurgence of the membership and their activity,

Martin was able to implement stronger security by adding more guards to each office around the continent. The Denver location, in particular, now had a rotation of sixty different guards, three groups of twenty covering various eight-hour shifts to protect the organization's top leadership and Council.

Duane remained heavily guarded within his holding cell, only permitted to roam outside of his room for one hour each day, which he typically spent pacing laps around the office with three guards behind him each step of the way. They had become so bustling with staff, much like Martin remembered upon his first visit, that no one paid any attention to Duane as he moseyed around the room like a depressed loner. He spoke few words and refused any conversations with Martin or Gerald.

While the main population of Road Runners moved forward with hope, Martin and Gerald spent their days with a cloud of distress hanging above their heads. They still had no idea where Chris was located, where Sonya had gone, or what to expect in the coming days. They had sent out all agents to try and solve these matters, but no one returned any answers, or even so much as a potential lead to follow.

Chris and Sonya were as good as erased from the planet. The uncertainty plagued Martin like an infectious disease. Sleep had become impossible, a growing belief that the moment he closed his eyes, the entire office would go up in flames. Eating became more of a chore than pleasure, Martin often poking at his food to make it appear like he had eaten more than just a couple bites.

He and Gerald spent each day in his office, a map of the continent thrown up on the screen and a stack of files from all the research that had been conducted on Chris and his movements over the last twenty years. Surely there was a pattern they could track down, and turn that information into an educated guess as to where he might be. They sent agents to inspect areas with no luck. It had become a witch hunt with no witch. They even kept a close watch on likely places Chris would end up, mainly his Wealth of Time store in Nevada. All of the cars remained outside from the day they had wanted swipe Mario Webster, but there were still no signs of Chris. Just knowing the old bat's location would help Martin sleep at night, but until then, it was a constant cycle of stress and paranoia.

The screens hanging around the office walls were muted as they showed the now constant Road Runner news station. Reporters and anchors were back into the swing of their routines and eager to get back on the job during these trying and fascinating times for the organization. They were in the middle of a piece regarding life in isolation on one of their private islands, a hot topic since everyone had the chance to witness the trial and sentencing of Councilwoman Murray.

The screens flickered, and Martin noticed out of the side of his vision, his stomach immediately hollowing out. He knew what the flicker meant and what came after it.

"Jesus Christ," he whispered, closing the laptop on his desk and not breaking his gaze from the screen directly across from him. Gerald sat back and followed his stare to the TV flickering out of control, like it had lost signal.

"Chris?" Gerald muttered under his breath, prompting a nod in response from Martin.

The stream of the virtual island completely gave way to a dark backdrop and Chris's face and frosty hair, popping off the screen in bright, crystal-clear resolution.

"Good afternoon, Road Runners," Chris said, keeping a stern

face. "I hope this message finds you doing well and hopeful. For years we have been fighting with each other, destined to do this until the end of time. For years it seemed that us here at the Revolution could have our way with the Road Runners. We land a punch, and you only return a slap on the wrist. I'll admit, things looked over for you when that little Vegas hotel went *ka-boom*! But now you have the fearless Martin Briar as your leader.

"I don't suppose Martin ever mentioned how weak-minded he is during all of his campaign promises? Martin is a man who follows his heart and not his conscience. And while there's no issue with that in particular, it should be alarming for the leader of a big organization like yours. Did you know Martin failed a mission to kill my daughter, Sonya, all because he couldn't bring himself to kill the woman he loved? I'm still here, kicking and screaming, all thanks to Martin Briar.

"And what did he do after I killed his mother? He went to hide in the Bahamas, getting drunk on the beach every night. What will he do now when times are tough? Go swim with the dolphins in the Maldives? I've enjoyed our years of battle, but it seems our war is coming to an end. You have the wrong leader at the exact wrong time. Yes, he destroyed my mansion, but can he handle what's coming next?"

Chris leaned back in his seat and turned his face away from the screen, mouthing to someone in the distance. He leaned forward and continued. "I have a surprise for you, Martin."

He waved his arm, and they watched as another body came into view and sat down, long blond hair swinging from side to side.

"Holy shit!" Martin gasped.

"Say hello to Sonya," Chris cackled as his daughter came into clear focus on the screen. "I was able to find her and bring her back to safety, out of danger from the Road Runners who want to kill her for their own gain. I love my daughter, but—and she'll admit this and understands—I love the Revolution more. Sonya and I had a falling out many years ago after my wife's death, leaving me with nothing but the Revolution. The Revolution is my family, even more than my dearest Sonya. I have a proposal for you, *Commander,* so I hope you're listening.

"I'm not afraid to get my hands dirty to ensure the Revolution continues as strongly as ever. I'm prepared to kill Sonya and pass along my 'gift' to someone else to carry. I've had a lengthy discussion with Sonya regarding this decision, and while she doesn't agree, she understands. You can go now, dear." Chris turned his head to Sonya as she stood and walked out of the screen's view.

During this quick pause Martin turned to Gerald and said, "Get in touch with the Nevada team right now and see if they've had any sighting of Mario Webster coming out of that building."

Gerald nodded and stepped out of the office. Martin caught a quick glimpse of all the frozen faces and stares in the bullpen, watching the televisions mounted around the entire room. Chris took a swig of water and finished speaking.

"Sonya's life is now in your hands, Mr. Briar. Bring me Duane and I will release Sonya. I'm in a small town called Three Creek, Idaho, just along the southern border of the state. We're the only house in town, so it shouldn't be hard for you to find us. I don't want any trouble. Bring Duane, and you can leave in peace. Sonya will be freed, but I can't say for certain where she'll go. You can save her life, Martin."

Chris leaned into the camera so that his face filled the entire screen. Wrinkles spread across his face as a grin revealed his yellow teeth. He started giggling, then opened his mouth to howling laughter, his uvula jiggling out of control before the screen cut black.

"Goddammit!" Martin barked, banging a fist on top of his desk. Gerald returned, slamming the door behind him and shaking his head.

"They haven't seen anyone come in or out of that store in three days. You don't suppose it's all a decoy of some sort?"

Martin shook his head ferociously. "Not the store. The store is everything. It's where Chris makes his Juice and pills, and does all of his experiments in his back lab."

"It's possible all of those Revolters went into the store and traveled to another time."

Martin scrubbed the top of his head with a balled fist, sending his hair into wild directions, as if he had been electrocuted. "That's probably what's happened. We can expand our search for that location throughout different years, but what are we really chasing? It's not even Chris in there, just his friend."

"Well, we know Chris is back in 2020. Should we even bother meeting with him?"

"I think we should," Martin said. He leaned forward to plant his elbows on the desk, folding his hands below his chin and gazing to Gerald with a look of madness and desperation in his eyes. "How would you feel about leading the mission to rescue Sonya?"

28

Chapter 28

The next morning, while Sonya sat at the kitchen table poking at a plate of scrambled eggs and bacon, Chris entered with a tall glass decanter of lime-green fluid. "Look what I got for you last night," he said with a smirk, his eyes studying his daughter like a hawk.

"Juice?!" she asked, stopping mid-chew on a piece of bacon.

"Bingo! Your ticket out of here once everything is complete."

She fought the urge to lunge out of her chair, snatch the bottle, and bolt out the front door. She wouldn't make it more than fifty feet before one of her father's newly imported guards tackled her to the ground.

"I've done my part. You showed me to Martin," she said. "Why can't I go now?"

Chris shook his head. "I wish it were that simple, dear. Martin isn't going to hand over Duane until he sees you're safe. If you're gone, then we just stand here at an impasse and we all die—except me, of course. I'm not willing to sacrifice Duane in order to kill Martin, although it is tempting. Killing Martin only does so much for our cause—he would just be replaced by someone else that same day, and back into the cycle we go. Round and round and round." Chris twirled a finger in circles like a musical conductor.

"And you really think this is going to work? That by some miracle, your goons will be able to capture Martin from whatever kind of crew he's going to arrive with?"

"More are coming," Chris said, placing the Juice on the counter next to the stove. Sonya glared at it, positioned close enough to tempt her, but just far enough to know better. Grease splattered the wall behind the bottle, and Sonya dropped her gaze to the cast-iron skillet she had used to cook the bacon, idle on the stove.

I could do it. Bash him on the head, grab the bottle, and run.

Chris shifted his weight and leaned toward the counter to block her view of the bottle behind his thin frame. "By tonight, we will have forty soldiers in this house, and each one will be ready for whatever Martin decides to bring. They'll hide, and we'll give the appearance that we don't have a very big operation going on here. Who would think any differently in this little house? It will lax them just enough for us to pounce, wipe out their entire crew and snatch Martin like a little kid falling for the stranger in a van with a cute puppy. And *you're* the puppy." Chris snickered as he crossed his arms and waited for a response from Sonya.

She said nothing, only shaking her head in disgust that her own father still insisted on using her as bait in his twisted games.

"It will all be over soon, dear," he said. "I just need you to trust me."

"Trusting you is nearly impossible."

"Say what you will, I've never harmed you and never will."

205

Chris walked away from the counter, daring Sonya to make an attempt on the bottle. Hell, she could even take a swig and will herself to one hundred years in the past. That would be more efficient than trying to run. Chris circled the room, taking slow, steady steps around the table. Sonya didn't understand how exactly forty more people were going to fit in the house—let alone hide. It was like asking an elephant to hide in a fish tank.

"There will soon be a day when this is all over," Chris said. "The Road Runners will no longer exist and you can roam the world freely. My question to you, dear, is what do you want out of that future life? Do you even remember what it feels like to truly be free and not have to constantly watch over your shoulder?"

"Gee, *Dad*, I don't know, since *you* made my life this way."

Now she folded her arms, the Juice a distant memory for the time being. Here he was again trying to rattle her brains, but why? He had her in the house with no viable escape route until he handed over that bottle—

—*Or I take it*—

—and he still toyed with her conscience like an evil kid frying ants with a magnifying glass.

"Sonya, if I never made you this way—created this bond with my blood—you'd have been dead a long time ago."

"No, I wouldn't have, because if you never made me this way, the Road Runners would have no reason to want me dead."

"Ahh, but there it is, don't you see? What happens to disloyal people who go running to the Road Runners?" Chris slashed his pointer finger across his throat, following the gesture with a cold wink.

"I have no doubt you'd kill me, but you'd never be able to catch me in that scenario."

Chris threw his head back and howled, clutching his hands over his gut. "Catch you, dear? I can do that in my sleep."

"Then you need to prepare to let me go. For good. I'll do whatever you ask for this sham trade you're staging, but after that, I hope you can respect my wishes and let me live in peace."

"You know I can never truly let you wander the world on your own. You are my lifeline, and I need to at least know you're alive and well. Unfortunately, the invincibility does not pass to you, so I can't afford to *not* know if you're alive."

Sonya nodded. "I can check in with you once a week. We can set a day of the week for me to call you to let you know everything is fine."

Chris let his smirk fall to the way side and scratched his chin. "We can maybe work something out like that. Honestly, it's hard to know what our world is going to look like after this upcoming encounter."

But don't you know already? Sonya wondered. Chris never made decisions without taking a peek into the future to see how it would all turn out. That method, however, wasn't foolproof. Any tweaked action in the present time could alter the course of the future, much like a cruise liner adjusting their course by one degree could put them on an entirely different continent than originally planned.

Chris surely had a sense how things would end up after Martin and his crew arrived to trade Duane. Was his reluctance to let Sonya live a truly free life a result of what was to come? Would it not end up being the victory parade that he had hoped for, but something much less? It certainly wasn't going to make matters worse for the Revolution, or else he wouldn't proceed with this plan.

"Is there something you're not telling me?" Sonya asked her

207

father, burning a gaze into his blue eyes.

He met her stare—a skill he had mastered when facing off with anyone—and shook his head. "I don't know what you mean. I've told you everything that's about to happen. What more do you want?"

She squinted her eyes, holding that cold, unforgiving stare. "You just seem less organized with this. I don't know why."

"I'm plenty organized, dear. Things feel hectic in this little shack we now live in, but I'm still very much in control."

Sonya broke her gaze and looked down to her plate, the remains of her scrambled eggs waiting to be devoured. She wondered if he really was in control. It was no secret that Chris was known for making erratic decisions and acting on impulse for revenge and violence instead of sound logic. Duane was the glue that held the Revolution together and prevented them from becoming an organized crime mob. Duane was the anchor who kept Chris grounded in reality, and also the compass that kept them on course for their long-term goals.

Martin and the Road Runners may have not realized—nor Chris, for that matter—but Duane's absence was directly contributing to a slow and steady unraveling of the Revolution and its leader, the Keeper of Time. Duane left and a Warm Soul became the leader of the Road Runners, followed by a resurgence in their once swayed confidence. With Duane gone, Chris dropped the protective fortress around his mansion in a cocky and reckless decision. Duane may have not been able to keep Martin out of power, but they would certainly be meeting in the Alaskan mansion right now had he never left.

Who would have thought a sick, old woman 5,000 miles away from Alaska would lead to the downfall of the Revolution?

Sonya smirked at the thought. She didn't wish harm on any

of those she had grown close to over her life, but it had always been clear that the Revolution contributed nothing substantial to the world besides pain and suffering for innocent people. Sonya wouldn't aid in the end of the Revolution, but also had no plans to intervene with its pending collapse.

Chris sat in the driver seat, a lunatic in control with no awareness of what was truly happening in the rest of the vehicle. Duane was the instructor in a student-driver vehicle, where he could take control of the wheel if the car started swerving out of control.

Sonya wondered if Martin knew all of this. Had he put in the time to really extract information from Duane and realize that he was the one calling the shots? Would Duane even speak? He had his frustrations with Chris, sure—much like a babysitter grows irritable when a child refuses to listen—but he remained loyal. Sonya didn't doubt that for one second. Duane would never betray the Revolution, even if his life was on the line. Without ever saying it aloud, Sonya knew Duane believed the Revolution could one day return to its roots as innocent time travelers only interested in making money and learning as much history as possible. There was only one person in the way, and he stood across from Sonya in the kitchen at this current moment.

Chris studied Sonya as she stared down to her plate in deep thought. She felt his deceitful eyes on her, but refused to give him the satisfaction of acknowledgment. Ever since she was a young girl trying to piece life together with no mother, she had learned to tune out the world around her—particularly her father who had always been trying to rile a reaction from her.

It'll all be over soon. One way or another.

She grinned as she picked up her fork and finished the rest of her breakfast, Chris leaving the kitchen without another word, clutching the Juice bottle in hand.

29

Chapter 29

The jet touched down in Twin Falls, Idaho, carrying Gerald, Duane, and six Road Runner soldiers armed and ready. They had scouted the area ahead of time with satellite imagery, and found the tiny house on the map.

Gerald deemed the location too small for Chris to have a small army of soldiers like he did in Alaska. This was a remote area that suggested peaceful negotiations over blunt force, but Gerald knew better.

Peace didn't – and couldn't – exist with Chris Speidel involved, and no matter how much he tried to give that appearance, the old man always had a trick up his sleeve. During the flight, Duane sat in the corner by himself, gazing out the window as if he were longing for his arrival to a tropical vacation. Gerald sat in the middle, his handpicked crew circled around him. The plans were already set after a heated discussion in Martin's office.

Gerald made his diligent attempt to persuade Martin into dropping a bomb on the little house. It could have been done by a helicopter, since there were no lay citizens anywhere near the property. But with Sonya inside the house, Martin refused. Gerald pushed the matter further, saying the war could end today if they did this, but Martin never budged.

He momentarily wondered if Martin was somehow working with Chris and Sonya, but dismissed the thought after remembering what Chris had done to Martin's mother. There was simply no forgiving that sort of action. *Even if promised a lifetime of invincibility?* he thought. Could Martin Briar actually set his personal grievances aside to the most evil man known, for a promise of never dying? Such an offer was impossible to completely eliminate, but Gerald still doubted any of it to be true.

By the time they arrived in Idaho and packed into a van for the hour-long drive south, Gerald was already playing through the exchange in his mind. They had all expected it to be straightforward. Gerald releases Duane, Chris releases Sonya, and everyone goes their separate ways. That was the agreement Martin and Chris had come to over the phone.

Only Chris didn't know Martin wasn't coming, a move suggested by Gerald in this evolving chess match of the minds. No matter what Chris said, Gerald didn't want their new commander so much as in the same state as the Keeper of Time. He'd seen it plenty of times in the future: it only took five seconds for your life to change. Five seconds of Martin on the same property as Chris was five too many.

The old bastard was surely angling to snag Martin, and would have no choice but to make a peaceful transaction with Gerald. If Gerald went missing on this mission, Martin had plans in place to rip the house apart until he was found.

The car ride, much like the flight, was mostly silent. No one wanted to discuss plans in front of Duane, in case he decided to blurt something aloud when facing Chris. They had discussed taping his mouth, but Martin didn't want them to seem too criminal in their handling of Duane.

In a private meeting Gerald held between just him and his crew, they all griped about why they couldn't at least make an attempt on Sonya's life. She would be right there for the taking. A couple of well-timed shots and the Revolution, as they knew it, would be done for good.

"There is unfortunately no scenario where I can defend any of you in front of the commander if Sonya Griffiths dies at your hands. She was once an integral part of the Road Runners until Commander Strike made an attempt on her life. Commander Briar would like to see her return to her role. He believes that if we can get Sonya back on our team, she can help us devise a way to kill Chris. I can't stop you from killing Sonya, but know if you do, your punishment will be harsh."

Gerald offered this explanation, knowing the truth was merely a ridiculous love story gone awry. Some had nodded, while others shook their head. All that mattered now, a few minutes away from Chris's new dwelling, was that they were all on the same page. Bringing Sonya home was the ultimate goal, aside from surviving, of course. They also understood there was virtually no chance of Sonya agreeing to return with them, and they were not to use force to make her do so. Gerald was the skilled negotiator in the group and would do everything in his power to persuade her to join them on the trip back to Denver.

The van started to slow as they pulled off the highway and onto a dirt road. Gerald had grown painfully bored with the scenic route of dirt and desert as far as they could see, an occasional tumbleweed dragging itself across the road, begging to be squashed by a tire.

"We're here," the driver announced, coming to a complete stop fifty yards away from a lone house. It had white adobe exterior, a couple of dead bushes scattered along the side of the home, while a cactus stood tall in the background.

Gerald stepped out of the van first, kicking the dirt under his boots into little clouds as he patted the pistol tucked into his belt. He remained beside the van, not wanting to venture too far onto Chris's turf without his highly skilled crew beside him.

"Let's roll," Gerald commanded over his shoulder.

The rest of the van doors slid open, everyone piling out. Duane was last, one of the soldiers escorting him as his hands were cuffed behind his back. Gerald wondered if Duane realized he could now make a run for the house. They would gain nothing by shooting him dead, likely signing their own death certificates on the spot.

Duane made no such move, content with letting this exchange take place as planned. Chris barged out of the house, the creaky screen door slamming back with a jolting smack.

"Good afternoon, Road Runners. How are we all doing today?" Chris sneered as he marched toward their group, three soldiers appearing from the side of the house with guns drawn as they joined their leader by his side.

Gerald and the rest of his crew all immediately whipped their guns out and held them toward the Revolters.

"Let's settle down," Chris said in a soft voice, patting the air downward with his hands. "No gunfire needs to happen today—this is just a clean transaction, right?"

"Let's keep it that way," Gerald demanded.

Chris stopped a few feet away and studied the group in front of him, a natural grin spreading across his face when his eyes met those of his closest friend. "Duane, good sir, I'm sorry you fell into this predicament. We'll have you back on our side and things can return to normal in no time."

Duane said nothing, letting his gaze fall to the ground.

"Where is Martin?" Chris asked, looking around as if he had somehow missed him in the group.

"We would never bring our leader to join a fist fight with you," Gerald said, stepping forward, no more than two feet between him and the lunatic known as Chris Speidel.

"Well, that was not part of the agreement," Chris snapped. "I specifically asked for Martin Briar to be part of this." He crossed his arms and frowned.

"We don't care about your demands, Chris," Gerald said. "We have Duane, you have Sonya. This is an easy exchange that doesn't require anyone else to be present."

"I wanted to speak with Martin in person. I *hate* when people don't keep their word."

"Keep their word?" Gerald replied, tightening his grip on the pistol. "Where's Sonya? Is she even here, or was that all a bunch of bullshit to try and trap Martin?"

Chris giggled like a child, his shoulders bouncing wildly. "So now you think *I'm* the liar?! Sonya is right inside. She's actually *here*, unlike your coward of a leader."

"Stop the sham, Chris," Gerald said. "We all know you wanted Martin here to take him. He blew your pathetic mansion to pieces and you couldn't bear the thought of letting him roam the world another day. I've been around a long time, and I'm from the future where you sick pigs rule the world—"

"Quite the beautiful world, don't you think?" Chris asked with a cheesy grin. "A place to raise a family . . . or lose one."

Gerald fought every nerve in his body from reaching out and

215

strangling this old shitbag with his bare hands. That would surely land a dozen bullets throughout his torso. "So what are we doing?" he asked instead, teeth gritted. "Martin's not here, so is the deal off? We're glad to take Duane back with us and squeeze all the info we can out of him."

"Duane would never talk to you people—that much I know. If Martin can't be here, then we have nothing further to discuss. You can leave Duane, and I'll let Sonya free."

"Show her to me first."

"Certainly." Chris half-bowed before turning around and starting toward the house. His goons remained in position. "Take them out, boys!"

Gerald had half a second to react, jerking his pistol toward the three Revolters and firing in sync with them also shooting at him and the crew. A dozen gunshots cracked the silent air within seconds of each other. The three Revolters collapsed to the ground, while one of Gerald's soldiers did the same, blood spreading from their chest like an oil spill. Just as he had crouched down to tend to his injured Road Runner, the slightest of rumbles came from the ground, as if a stampede of wild rhinos were trampling down the nearby highway.

Everyone kept their weapons cocked and ready, heads spinning around as it wasn't quite clear where the rumbling was coming from. Chris had completely vanished inside, where Gerald would never see him again.

"Holy shit!" one of his soldiers screamed, flailing as he tried to run back into the van. What sounded like an entire case of fireworks exploding was actually a shower of bullets coming from the nearly three dozen Revolters running from the backyard and around the house.

Gerald fired his pistol, but knew this was it. They were grossly outnumbered and had zero chance of escaping. Out of all the tragedy he had managed to survive in the future, his life would end in a gunfight with the Revolters in the year 2020, well before the continent took its final turn to the point of no return. He only wished he had more time to process a thought. If he did, he would have thought back to his family and how lucky he was for finally getting the chance to see them again in the afterlife. He might have reflected on the outstanding success he had of surviving for so long in this ugly war. With even a split second to think, he would have made a wish that his own death wouldn't pass in vain, and that Martin would finally bring a swift end to this without him. The journey had been a fun, interesting ride, and he had often wondered what his life would have looked like had he never joined the Road Runners in the first place.

Unfortunately for Gerald, with his entire crew dead on the ground behind him, Duane spared and sprinting toward the house, he didn't have a moment to form any of these thoughts that many others experienced before their pending death. A slug caught him square in the forehead, along with three others, and six more into his chest and stomach.

The last thing Gerald Holmes saw, as he collapsed to the dirt, was Chris Speidel standing in his doorway, cackling wildly with glee.

30

Chapter 30

Martin had experienced plenty more downs than ups over the course of his life. Now there was blood on his hands thanks to his direct authorization of a mission. Chris had taken the liberty of snapping a photo and sending it in a text message to Martin. The caption read: *Wish you were here!*

The picture showed the seven Road Runners splayed across the ground, dead as prairie dogs on the side of a highway. Blood was splattered across the white van behind the bodies, like a child had thrown a tantrum with a bucket of red paint.

"Gerald," Martin whispered to himself, unable to form a concrete thought about what his eyes were seeing. He received the text message an hour earlier and had promptly forwarded to an investigation team who was now on their way to the scene, with hopes of learning what had exactly happened via a helicopter above. They'd also attempt to identify the bodies as best they could with a super-zoom camera lens.

Word of the massacre hadn't yet reached the public, but it was only a matter of time. The lieutenant commander had been killed and there was no way of hiding that fact, especially with

Gerald so popular among the organization. Martin now had the unfortunate task of finding a replacement for his number two, a process he simply didn't have the energy for. He never had a real chance to mourn the loss of those closest to him, especially since joining the Road Runners. He had to deal with the major blows of Sonya's betrayal and the murder of his mother all on the fly, needing to keep moving forward to avoid a similar fate. Here he was again, his closest friend and confidant dead, Martin with no time to dwell on the fact, needing to rush into a decision for a replacement to ensure the continued safety of the entire Road Runner population.

At least when his mother died he was able to escape to the islands and live in a somewhat solitary manner, but now he'd have to face the organization as their leader, their beacon of hope in another dark time that had fallen upon them.

Martin's relationship with the members was already off to a whirlwind of a start, but they had seemed to turn a corner for the better in recent days. Would this failed mission lead to more calls for his removal from office? Would there be enough outrage for this to actually proceed to the next level of a review by the Council? What would the Council think of the hastily crafted mission, and the reasoning behind it? Gerald may have planned every detail, but Martin gave the final approval and authorization, making him equally responsible for the seven deaths. On the flip side, the organization might further unite behind Martin in these new, troubling times.

The screens in his office started to flicker. "No!" he whined, jumping out of his chair and running for the TV's as if he could stop them. He hoped he'd at least have the benefit of time to deliver the news to the Road Runners, not have it be mocked by Chris for the world to watch.

The feed of the Road Runner news network ended and was replaced by Chris Speidel, standing outside his new house, the sky a piercing blue behind his frosty head. He opened with a grin that showed his yellowing teeth. "Good afternoon, my dearest Road Runners. I'm back so soon, I know. My apologies for ruining your day, but I just wanted to make sure that you all know your 'commander' is not a man of his word. He and I had specific plans to meet and settle a debt. He refused to come and now there are seven dead Road Runners on my front lawn, your Lieutenant Commander Gerald Holmes being one of them."

Martin shook his head and buried his face into open palms.

"The transaction still took place, rest assured. Duane is back to safety with me, and Sonya has run free with her new bottle of Juice. But since your little commander wanted to make changes to the plans, I made some minor ones myself."

Chris spun his camera around to reveal a live shot of the dead bodies on his property. No one had been moved, including the van. The blood splatters had dried, turning to a shade of black. Chris skipped toward Gerald, who was closest to the house, and zoomed in on his dead face, gray eyes staring at the sky, lips still parted from the moment his final breath escaped.

Chris howled as he zoomed out, keeping the camera on Gerald, and started kicking the dead lieutenant commander in the side.

"You see," Chris said, jerking the camera back to his face. "This is what you get when you don't follow through on your word. I'm a simple man—I don't ask for much beyond your honesty and integrity. These dead bodies are *your* fault, Mr. Briar. And to the rest of you Road Runners, how much more can you take? Can't you see that your organization is slowly dying—literally—since Martin Briar took over? I can't say that I'm disappointed—your demise is my ultimate goal. I just wished I was the one to end it instead of yourselves. Before you think about ever destroying one of my properties again, remember this image."

The camera swung back around to Gerald and jerked through the air like a documentary cameraman running from a pack of lions. The view settled on Gerald's head, promptly stomped repeatedly by Chris's foot. His head rolled back and forth, a new pool of blood spreading on the ground beneath. This image played for ten seconds while Chris continued roaring with laughter before the feed died and returned to a stunned Road Runner news anchor.

The news feed cut to black, leaving the collective Road Runner organization in silence. Martin's cell phone buzzed immediately, a call from the United Kingdom that he quickly answered.

"Martin, what the hell is going on over there?" Commander Blair spewed through the phone. "Is this some kind of joke?!"

"None of this is a joke," Martin replied calmly, despite his heart drumming like a rabid monkey trying to break out of a cage. "We've reached the tipping point in this war."

"Bullshit! The tipping point was when that hotel collapsed like a fucking Jenga tower. We've all seen what the future in your country looks like—why are you not doing anything to stop it?!"

"I have been. This is what I've been trying to tell you—we need help!"

The cell phone trembled in Martin's shaky grip, adrenaline, rage, and sorrow all swirling in an emotional cocktail, blasting through his body. He wanted to cry as much as he wanted to reach into the phone and shake Blair by his throat to get the point across. And now, with his top strategist another casualty in this horrendous war, Martin felt alone on an island with no idea how to get off. This was the price the Road Runners would pay for forcing him to run in the election. Whether or not they had a bigger plan at play now seemed irrelevant. Enough lives had been lost in the few weeks since Martin took control that he now questioned if it was all his fault. Running off to a hidden island to hide like cowards no longer seemed like such a wild idea. Surely the supporters of Yohan Templeton were somewhere shaking their heads, cursing Martin's name.

"Help is not coming, Commander," Blair said, his voice calming down to a normal, but morbid, tone. "We've all had conversations about sending help your way, but it's just too dangerous. High risk, low reward from our viewpoint."

"Saving the lives of the *millions* of Road Runners on this continent is *low reward*?!"

"It's not about saving lives. All Road Runners are valuable. But without Commander Quang on board, none of us want to risk our smaller pool of soldiers. Especially since we still don't have an actual plan to take down Chris. Understand that we look at all the numbers: how quickly he recruits new Revolters, how often. He has only tapped into one percent of the entire population on the continent. Even if we managed to wipe out half of his force, they'd be replenished in no time. There's nothing we can do to stop him right now, so there's no reason for us to get involved in a fight that has no foreseeable end."

The one thing Martin had learned he could always count on from his fellow commanders was their dedication to morality. Even knowing that killing Sonya could be the move to slingshot them to an end of this madness, they respected the fact that she was still technically a Road Runner and therefore should not be sacrificed. No matter how ugly the situation became.

"So that's it?" Martin asked, tossing his free hand in the air while he paced around his office. "The rest of our so-called Road Runners will just watch our demise on TV like it's a fucking action movie. What was the point of this call if you're not offering *anything*?"

"The point is to let you know to stay calm. It's a bad time, yes, but it's only seven deaths. In the big picture, that's minimal and you can still recover and make a move."

Martin shook his head. *Only seven deaths.* "Fuck you," he seethed before hanging up the call and throwing his cell phone at the wall, sending an explosion of plastic shards in every direction. "Only seven deaths?!" Martin screamed to the ceiling, his entire body now trembling to match his hands. "Fuck!"

Tears rolled down his face as the urge to kill Chris had never been stronger. But he knew this is exactly what Chris wanted, an emotional knee-jerk reaction that would land Martin in a vulnerable spot where Chris would wipe him off the face of the Earth, just as he had done to his mother. As much as the desire throbbed for him to hop on the jet and fly to Idaho right now, it would have to wait.

"I'm going to kill you, you son of a bitch! For Sonya, for my mom, for Gerald. And for bribing me into this bullshit life."

Martin returned to his desk and pulled open his bottom drawer, bringing out a bottle of whiskey and drinking directly from it. The time to make a final plan for the removal of Chris Speidel now loomed on the horizon, but first he wanted to numb the pain and mourn the loss of his closest friend.

223

31

Chapter 31

Three days later, while Martin traveled to Chicago in the year 2064 for Gerald's funeral, the Council convened after taking the last couple of days off to mourn the lieutenant commander's life. Gerald may have been the number two in charge, but he had touched the lives of everyone within the organization, even more so since running in the campaign with Martin.

All of the new Council members had direct ties to Gerald, working with him in some capacity at another point in time, earning them personal recommendations for their new jobs. If anything, Chief Councilman Uribe was the least familiar with Gerald on a personal basis, but still understood the grueling loss this was for the organization. Gerald was likely a lock to succeed Martin in the commandership, as was often the case, but this now marked consecutive administrations of death falling upon the number two position. Losing Bill was a tough blow, especially once all of the details came out about Julian's corruption, but he lacked the 'it' factor that Gerald had. When Gerald Holmes walked into a room, he demanded attention and respect, yet was friendly with everyone he spoke with. He was versatile as a man, as a Road Runner, and would never be replaced.

With all of this heavy in their hearts, the Council met for the first time since his death and it was naturally their topic of discussion for the first hour. Once they settled down and Uribe called for an official start to the day, a sense of business-as-usual returned to their chambers. The chatter died down and Uribe addressed his Council, still lacking one member as they waited for Yohan Templeton to decide if he wanted to join as the replacement to Councilwoman Murray.

"Ladies and gentlemen, these are difficult times. Considering what we know about the future, it's safe to say that we have reached the crossroads. We can either continue the path we're on and arrive promptly to our doomed destination, or we can take swift action today to swerve out of our current lane and head for safety. We've had plenty of teams study our future and how we arrive there, and honestly, it's impossible to pinpoint an exact event that leads us down the dark path. I'm taking the liberty to claim that this is it. And based on my email inbox from the last three days, you might agree with me. I've received over 1,000 emails since the attacks in Idaho, and each one is calling for Martin's head—some even for *our* heads.

"The important thing to remember in a time like this is that we are all in this together: us and Commander Briar. Perhaps even more so than in the past. For this Council, we're in a tough position, there's no denying it. We need to make the decision to kill Sonya Griffiths, and please know it will be met with a ton of rage from our commander. We will take some heat, but it's the tough decision that's been on hold for far too long. We have the power to make it happen and utilize all of our resources

225

to do so. Our main objective will be trying to get Commander Briar on our side. We must move forward as a unified team."

Uribe stopped and took a sip of water, gesturing with his arm for anyone to speak up regarding the matter.

"Does this mean we're voting on something right now?" Councilwoman Dawson asked. "I'm confused as to what exactly you're asking of the Council."

"I don't want to vote until we've completely discussed Sonya," Uribe said. "Does anyone here oppose a motion to assassinate Sonya Griffiths?"

They all looked around at each other, a heavy silence filling the room that might as well have spoken on their behalf. Sonya was still a Road Runner, but they no longer had an issue sacrificing her life in exchange for the greater good.

"I'm glad we're on the same page," Uribe said after thirty seconds of awkward glances around the chambers. "Now, once we put this to a formal vote on the record, the order will be live to complete the assassination. But that's where we may run into issues. While we can authorize an attack, we have no oversight in administering the attack—that needs to be completed by either a commander or their lieutenant."

"So we're at an impasse?" Councilman Bolt asked.

"Not necessarily. Like I said, this is where it gets tricky. Is there some sort of deal we can put together for Commander Briar that might sway him to move this all forward? We know he's opposed to the thought of any harm falling upon Sonya, but he has to realize we're eventually headed to that decision. Whether it's with him as commander, or after he's gone, someone is going to advance this and see it through."

"Are you talking about threatening him? Political blackmail?" Councilman Bolt asked.

"Of course not, we're not the American government. We don't need to use force to push this through. I have an idea, but want to hear yours first. Let's see what we can come up with."

"I don't see why we need to apply any pressure in this matter," Councilwoman Barns said. "Does he not see the inevitable future? If we do nothing, the membership is going to eventually secure the numbers for a recall vote. Then how do we look if we decide to keep him in power?"

"That's exactly what we're trying to avoid," Uribe said. "That will most certainly be the end result if we stand pat. The last thing I want this young Council to have to worry about is being forced into such a polarizing decision. It's no fun, but that's why I want a proactive approach. Let's find some middle ground with the commander and avoid that whole mess."

"Then we should just tell him the facts," Barns replied. "No point in beating around the bush."

"The facts will be laid out for him to consider, but this is a matter of the heart, not politics. Remember, our commanders don't run for re-election."

"Let's just enforce the law," Councilman Bolt said from the opposite end of the table.

"In what sense?" Uribe asked.

"Section seven, article thirteen of the Bylaws. '*The Council reserves the right to hold in contempt any Road Runner who does not act within any approved rulings by the Council. This statute has no limitations, and any disciplinary actions toward executive members must pass with a unanimous vote before enacted.*' If we vote to assassinate Sonya, and Commander Briar refuses to move forward with a thoroughly planned attack, we can exercise this power and threaten the commander with removal from office, or even imprisonment—that would be up to us."

"That sounds like a strong-arm move," Councilwoman Penny said. "I don't think that's what we're going for here."

Uribe slunk back in his seat and propped a fist under his chin. Of course he knew about the particular rule in the Bylaws, but he didn't expect a new Councilor with virtually no experience to remember those two sentences out of the entire document. It was buried within a massive text, but Councilman Bolt had clearly done some homework with his couple of days off.

"It may seem like a brutal move," Bolt said, leaning forward and planting his elbows on the table. "But it's a rule, and I believe it was written for a reason. I trust that our founders did extensive research on different governmental systems all throughout the past and future, and crafted the Bylaws around their findings. Our current setup only allows us so much power, and rightfully balances it with the commander. But should the entire organization be put at risk because of an emotional whim from Commander Briar? Call me crazy, but I think this rule was meant for exactly this situation."

"I think we need to try a more civil approach first," Penny said. "Maybe we bring him into the chambers and let him know what exactly is going on. I can't imagine he's not seeing this for himself, or that it will be some surprise when we bring it up. Last time I spoke with Gerald he told me that this has been a topic of discussion nearly every day."

"What do you think, Chief Councilman?" Bolt asked. "What was your idea?"

All heads turned to Uribe, who sat up stiffly again.

"I think we can pull a little bit of everything and use it in a discussion with Commander Briar. He'll be back tomorrow morning, and I think we need to hash this all out immediately. As for my idea . . . it's a bit unethical, perhaps, but it may be necessary, as I don't think even the threat of imprisonment will be enough to nudge him in the right direction. I want to float the idea of telling him that Sonya personally killed Gerald."

The chambers fell silent again, many faces scrunching while other bodies squirmed in their seats.

"Is that legal?" Bolt asked.

"Like I said, it's unethical. But from what I've gathered, not illegal. Investigation reports change quite a bit as information is gathered. I've already spoken with the head of this particular investigation, and they have assured me the report can state this simple fact for the time being. Keep in mind, there was a lot of gunfire during this attack, and it hasn't yet been determined for sure who shot Gerald. It's presented us this unique opportunity with a small window of time to push it through as truth."

"I don't know, this sounds like something that can come back and haunt us," Penny said, shifting in her seat.

"All paperwork will suggest that we're making a decision based on the information we have at this moment. We have at least three days before the investigative team updates any of their notes. Do we want to pursue this option?"

The chambers remained silent for a few more seconds while each Councilor fidgeted with their writing utensils and gazed around like they were looking at the stars. No one opposed, yet no one voiced support, either. Everyone understood the gravity of the current predicament the Road Runners were now under, and they needed an aggressive, all-hands-on-deck approach if they wanted any hope of coming out of this alive.

"Let's do it," Councilwoman Dawson finally said. "All of it. The lie, the threat, the law. Throw it all at him and see what happens."

Uribe looked around to the others, all of them nodding in agreement, but not speaking. "You know we are off the record. We can discuss this openly. No need to fear any backlash. I'm not turning on the microphone until we're ready to formally cast a vote. Now, with that said, does anyone have an objection? We need to all be on the same page."

Councilman Bolt spoke first. "I think if we use all of the options discussed, we'll get the action we need. What's important to remember is that this is bigger than all of us. Whatever happens in the next six months is going to forever shape the future of our organization. We have arrived to the critical swinging point of our history. We either go all-in with our decision, or we start counting down our final days. Does anyone feel otherwise? I know we've all studied the past and future quite extensively."

"This feels wrong, and I suppose it always will," Council-woman Penny said, shaking her head. "But if our survival depends on it, will anyone really care? We don't have two years to wait for a new commander who might be willing to agree to this. We can't even say where Sonya will be in two years, let alone right now. We can approve this decision today, get Commander Briar on board, and it still won't mean anything until we can actually find Sonya. She has Juice again and will stay on the run. I doubt she tries to settle in any one location for too long."

"So are you saying you approve?" Uribe asked, raising his eyebrows.

"I don't agree with it, but this is bigger than me—bigger than all of us. So I will vote yes for the greater good."

"Councilwoman Penny raises a good point. This entire plan rests in the hands of those looking for Sonya. We'll have to authorize two missions, one being the assassination of Sonya Griffiths, but first, an all-out manhunt for her. It's a desperate move, but one that's necessary."

"Will it require cooperation from any other commanders?" Bolt asked.

"No. We have our own Road Runners who live on other continents. I doubt any other commander will let us use their local members, even for a simple mission like tracking a person down. Does anyone else have anything to add, or shall we vote?"

Uribe scanned the table and waited a full minute until reaching forward and flicking on a switch next to his microphone protruding from the table.

"This is Chief Councilman Uribe, notating the start of our daily session within the chambers in Denver, Colorado. Today we are calling to vote an authorization to assassinate Sonya Griffiths. Reports show that she is responsible for the death of Lieutenant Commander Gerald Holmes. There are added benefits tied to her demise, including the opportunity to successfully end the life of Christopher Speidel. In addition, we will vote on a mission authorization to deploy every available resource toward finding Ms. Griffiths. We will begin by casting our votes anonymously. I will count and Councilwoman Barns will confirm. Councilors, please cast your votes for the authorization to assassinate Sonya Griffiths."

Each member scribbled their vote on a piece of paper that was then folded and pushed to the center of the table. Uribe had a sliver of doubt that an opposition vote would make its way into the pile. It wasn't like the Council to remain silent during a discussion, but this was a gray area that perhaps no one wanted the risk of their spoken words being recorded. They didn't need a unanimous decision to pass the authorization, but it would certainly look better to the public knowing their Council was in complete agreement about the matter.

Uribe collected the slips of paper once everyone was done, and quickly counted, relieved. "For the authorization of a mission to assassinate Sonya Griffiths, the Council has voted in favor, six votes to zero."

"Confirmed," Councilwoman Barns quickly said as she finished counting the slips that Uribe passed along to her.

"Councilors, please cast your votes for the authorization of deployment of all available North American Road Runners to find Sonya Griffiths."

They repeated the process, this time much quicker.

"For the authorization of deployment of all available Road Runners to locate Sonya Griffiths, the Council has voted in favor, six votes to zero."

"Confirmed."

"That settles our voting measures for the day. For the record, the authorization has passed for these two essential missions, however we still need to coordinate with Commander Briar the finer details on how this will be carried out. We will schedule a meeting with the commander for tomorrow morning, but it will be off the record, considering the confidential nature of such discussion. We will provide as many updates as possible. This concludes our morning session, we will meet back this afternoon to wrap up some smaller matters. The Council is now in recess."

Uribe flicked the microphone off and leaned back in his chair, nodding quietly to himself. It was easily the most unethical decision he had ever made during his tenure as a Councilor, but only the future would tell if it was the right call, and ultimately decide his own legacy.

32

Chapter 32

The next morning called for the meeting between Martin and the Council. He received a calendar invite to his phone while still in future Chicago, and quickly accepted it, dismissing it as nothing but a likely check-in between the two parties. He had no idea the Council was waiting to flip his world even more than it already had been.

Martin caught his return flight home to Denver after jumping back to 2020, his heart heavy after two days of mourning with those closest to Gerald. He had given Gerald's potential replacement no thought, not wanting to rush into a decision while teetering on the brink of depression. Perhaps that's what the Council wanted to help him with.

When he arrived in Denver, gray clouds dumped rain on the city, further continuing the melancholy that seemed to linger above the entire organization. Martin paid no attention, aside from watching streaks of rain drizzle along the car window as they rode back to the downtown office.

One month as Commander, he thought as they rode in silence, the car filled with its driver and three security guards. *Thou-*

sands of Road Runners and civilians dead, my number two wiped off the planet, and Sonya on the run again. This has to be the biggest failure of a commandership in the history of the organization, and it's only taken a month.

Being away from Denver for the funeral provided Martin plenty of time to think, and he couldn't force himself to shake off the urge of resigning from his position, and banishing himself to one of the private islands. If the pope was allowed to resign, then why not Martin? Was that something that had even been done in the past? What did that process look like, and how furious would everyone be if they needed to run a whole other election so soon?

The existence of the Road Runners—and time travel, in general—had pulled Martin out of the constant sorrow he lived in, revitalizing his life and delivering a new purpose. This had gradually snowballed into his current leadership position with the organization, leading him to this specific point in life right back where he had started: wishing for death to put an end to the madness.

He still longed for a world where Chris Speidel no longer existed, but the constant flow of negativity had extinguished any remaining fire within his soul to pursue it. Perhaps he'd go on a suicide mission and kill Chris himself, leaving the world with a great gift while ending his miserable existence once and for all.

The thought brought the first grin to his lips in a couple of days, just as the car parked in front of the office, prompting two of the guards to jump out of the car and head into the building first. The head of security called for a full revamp of their policies, implementing that two guards must walk ahead of the commander at all times when entering a new building, even the main headquarters. After Strike's disappearance and death, they had made a mandatory rule that the commander must always have at least two guards when stepping outside of the office. They upgraded the ruling to now include four guards, one of which must also be the driver for any trips across town.

Martin let himself out of the car, insisting to his team that he didn't need the door opened for him like he was the Queen of England. He followed his guards into the marketing office and into the basement where the bullpen remained silent since Gerald's untimely death.

Martin passed through with his head down, not in the mood for the usual small talk that accompanied his morning strolls through the office. He had less than an hour until his meeting with the Council, and planned to pass the time in his office, with the lights off. He surely had a pile of work, but lacked any energy to force his way through it. Besides, his main priority was to find a new number two, especially if he had plans of entering a life-threatening mission.

He closed the office door behind him and sat behind his desk, leaving his computer off and dropping his head on crossed arms. The silence was dizzying, and he felt all the eyes of the former commanders watching him from the wall in their 3x5 frames, judging him, mocking him, laughing at him.

You'll never hang on this wall with us! their collective voices shouted at him. *You disgraceful piece of shit! Are you sure you don't secretly work for the Revolution? Traitor!*

Martin's hands trembled with rage, prompting him to swipe the stapler that rested on the edge of his desk, and hurl it across the room. It crashed into the portrait of Commander Amanda Rodriguez, who led the organization from 1989-1990, cracking the glass before it fell from the wall and clattered to the floor, sending shards across the carpet.

"Fuck!" he barked, slamming a fist on to the desk. "Pull it together, Martin. Everything will work out—it always has."

Worked out, huh? Like your ex-wife killing your only child and tossing her body in the lake like a dead fish? Like your mother being killed all because of your decision to enter this life? Like all the innocent Road Runners who were minding their business that day in the hotel? Or like Sonya lying to you and running away? How is that happily-ever-after working out?

"Nothing has *ever* worked out," he said to assure himself. "We're gonna take things one week at a time. If one more bad thing happens this week, I'm leaving in the middle of the night. I'll rip my tracking device out and spend the rest of my life hiding from the bullshit. If I can actually go a week without someone in the organization dying, then I'll reconsider." As Martin spoke, he directed his words to the portrait of Commander Strike mounted next to his enlarged photo. She was the only familiar face on that wall, and somehow the only source of comfort in his luxurious office.

Nearly every day he had spent a moment wondering what life would be like had she never been kidnapped. He definitely wouldn't be the commander, but what would his role look like with the Road Runners? What happened after his term ended? All of these commanders hung on the wall, but he had never once heard about their recent activity. The unknowing churned his stomach, even though he still had twenty-three months left of his term.

Unless I make a run for freedom.

Martin shook his head, having enough of the negative thoughts swirling around, and checked the clock to see that his hour had quickly passed. He stood, slightly off-balance as he exited his office and started down the long hallway to the conference room that served as the Council's chambers. His feet shuffled along the floor, moving at a pace fast enough to keep anyone from striking up a conversation. A couple of eyes looked up at him, but no one really paid him any attention in the quiet bullpen.

Martin grew more tired with each passing second, and not in the sense of requiring sleep. He had slept on the jet ride to and from Chicago, and actually managed seven hours of sleep each night while in the Windy City. By all considerations, he was well-rested. It was a day off he needed. The constant bustle of his job crept up his body, inching toward his throat where it would suffocate and squeeze the life out of him. It surely didn't help having so much blood on his hands in a short matter of time. If he could just take one day to spend at his own house and do nothing but watch TV on the couch, he might feel better about life. But a day off was a long time away, especially with nobody to help run the organization in his absence.

Perhaps he could float the idea by the Council and see what they thought. He knocked on the door before pushing it open to find all of the Councilors in their seats around the oval table, Uribe at the head and waving an arm for Martin to join them. They had set up a chair next to Uribe, but a foot back from the table. Touching the table was an old tradition that could only be done by active Council members.

"Good morning, Commander," Uribe said as Martin made his way to the seat.

"Good morning, all." He offered a quick nod before sitting down and crossing his hands on his lap. "How is everyone doing?"

Uribe bobbed his head from side to side. "We're doing okay.

After a couple of days off we got back to work yesterday. It's a dark time for us all, but we have plenty to do to shape our future."

"I see. Is that what this meeting is about?"

"Yes, Commander. We voted on a couple of measures yesterday and would like to discuss them with you. I must warn you—you may not like what we have to say."

Martin squirmed in his seat and readjusted his posture by sitting more upright and crossing his arms over his chest. "Okay, let's hear it."

"Let me start by saying that our hands are tied. Since the attacks in Idaho, I've now received north of 5,000 emails from our members as of this morning. For context, we normally receive emails on a regular basis and see spikes after particular tragedies. During calm times, maybe ten emails a day. After Bill's death, we received 300 over the week. After Julian's death and revelation of his dirty deeds, we received maybe 500. After Strike's death, I read through 1,000 emails. Even the Vegas attack turned up 2,000 messages. But so far, we're at 5,000 in three days. There's essentially a new email every single minute."

"I didn't realize the membership could contact the Council. What are people saying?" Martin asked, leaning forward as he had no idea what to expect.

"Normally they make requests for new policies, and if we see enough of a general theme across the emails—say at least half of them calling for the same thing—then we'll discuss here in the chambers and decide how to move forward. Some matters require formal votes and signatures from the membership."

"Can you please tell me what's going on?" Martin asked in the most polite voice he could manage.

239

"Yes. The emails have all been calls for your removal. I suspect the membership has the votes needed for a recall. We don't want that. And honestly, they don't really want that, either. Underlying each ask for a recall is a desire to end the war. Our people have reached their wit's end—they don't care what it takes, just make it happen. They feel a new leader will be able to get the job done, perhaps someone more experienced. We took the liberty to discuss our options and voted to assassinate Sonya Griffiths."

Uribe paused and waited for a reaction from Martin, but his eyes remained fixated into the distance, blank and lifeless.

"We also approved an order to utilize all resources in finding her. We currently have no idea what year or location she may be in, but we have enough people to find her within the next month. Both measures were passed unanimously, and will now move to your desk for administration and implementation. We understand that Gerald would have been your go-to in this situation, but it's imperative you at least find someone with a strong strategic background to carry this out and provide some guidance."

"So this is it?" Martin asked, nearly mumbling. "The decision has been made for me."

He spoke more to himself than the Council, dropping his gaze to his fidgeting fingers in his lap.

"Commander, there are some sensitive details we had to consider before making this decision. We understand the nature of this and that you're opposed to killing Ms. Griffiths, but the initial investigative reports are showing that Sonya was the one who killed Gerald. She landed the shot."

Martin looked up, fighting to stay calm, but feeling dizzy again, the chambers spinning around him. "Sonya? I don't believe it."

"Whether or not you believe it doesn't change our team's findings. You need to decide if you're going to continue down this path of defending Sonya's life in exchange for the barrage of attacks we keep enduring from the Revolution—and now the Liberation, too."

"Oh, *I* get to decide? Because this sure as hell doesn't make it seem like it's *my* choice. What happened to not sacrificing a Road Runner, no matter what it could mean? Or does that only apply when it's convenient?"

"Commander, we can only work with the information we have. I don't agree with the initial decision by Commander Strike for that initial assassination attempt on Sonya, but that has since unraveled into this mess. I believe that decision is what cost Commander Strike her life. It scared Chris and he "He reacted. Must have thought Sonya was safe as a Road Runner and that her life would never be in danger, especially in her role as a recruiter. But that changed when they sent you to kill her."

"So since the Road Runners broke her trust, and sent her into hiding, that somehow justifies us killing her? My defense of Sonya is much more than my feelings for her. I've never seen someone treated so poorly. She dedicated her life to the Road Runners and *this* is how she gets repaid? You people act like she was working with Chris behind our backs, when in reality Strike just got greedy and made a hurried decision."

"To be fair to Commander Strike, rest her soul, she did not make that decision. It was a vote cast by all Lead Runners across the continent. It narrowly passed, and I think she regretted ever putting it up for a vote. She decided to go a different route to bypass the Council and see what the rest of the leadership wanted, then made her final decision from there. She could have just as easily decided against it—the vote wasn't binding like a Council vote—but there's no point in picking apart that process right now."

"Why didn't you stop it?" Martin snapped. "Surely you could have."

"We could, but the Council was equally as split. All this aside, Commander, our decision is unanimous and we need you to implement it."

Martin looked around the table and shook his head. "I can't believe you all. I personally chose each of you to serve on this Council, and this is how you vote?"

"Commander, if you can put your personal feelings aside, you'll see that this is what's best for the Road Runners at this time."

"Put my *feelings* aside? Forgive me for saying this, but my life has slowly been ripped apart since I joined the Road Runners, never mind what has happened since I became commander. The theme in my life since joining has been a constant cycle of getting my hopes up—even having my life headed in the right direction—only for everything to be ripped out from under me. This last month has easily been the most fucked-up month of my entire existence—and I've lived through the loss of my child at the hands of my *wife*, mind you."

"And that's exactly why we cast these votes, Commander. You're enduring enough on a daily basis. This decision didn't need to rest solely on your shoulders, especially with Gerald gone. We don't expect you to see clearly—we understand the hell you're being put through. At the same time, we're getting pressured from the public to do something, and we don't think removing you from office will actually solve anything. The time has come to end this war, and that's what we're dedicated to doing."

"And if I don't agree to any of this, will you just bypass me again? What's the point of having a commander if you guys do whatever you want?"

"No, we can't bypass. We don't have the authority to execute a mission, just to approve it. We do, however, have the power to hold you in contempt if you refuse to do the work presented to you by the Council. Remember, the Council represents the people, the commander represents the organization. This has always been the way it is, for both balance of power and clarity of functions, but there are plenty of times we must work together. Now is that time."

Martin snickered as he shook his head once more. "So you get to blackmail me into doing this? Fan-fucking-tastic. Congrats, Council, you win."

Martin stood up and stomped toward the door, stopping when Uribe shouted. "Commander Briar, stop right there!"

He pivoted and planted his hands on his hips, like a teenage girl upset that her parents wouldn't let her go out.

"Commander, we don't want to make any difficult decisions. This sort of matter can cause irreparable damage to the Council *and* the office of the commander, not to mention another split in our membership. We're willing to hear any of your concerns and come to an agreement on what this process will look like. At the end of the day, the decision on how this is all carried out is up to you as the commander. Can you at least work with us?"

Martin stood in silence, his lips pursed to give the appearance of deep thought. He knew this moment was a long time coming, he just didn't expect it to be made for him. Gerald had set the expectation that if he wanted to be the commander to bring peace to the Road Runners, then killing Sonya was the direct route to do that. He had wrestled with this privately ever since he had started campaigning, and knew it would all eventually come down to this.

Yes, Martin still had feelings for Sonya, but the reality that he had long been avoiding was that she did not feel the same. He felt a real connection during their six months together in 1996, and even back into 2018 when she returned with him. As much as she swore to playing along with their love story for the sake of luring him into the Road Runners, he believed she at one point had developed feelings for him, too. Regardless of how it all played out, she had been the one to fully drag him into this mess, he being a pawn in a war between a daughter and her deranged father on the opposite side of the fence.

Closure had helped him heal two decades after Izzy's disappearance, and perhaps closing the book on Sonya would also allow him to move forward in life and whatever remained in his final years on this planet.

"Don't worry about me," Martin said to the Council. "I'll do it."

He left the room without another word, leaving the Council in stunned silence.

33

Chapter 33

It only took three weeks for them to find Sonya. With all hands on deck, it was only a matter of time before they spotted her, blending into Chicago society in 1933, the peak of the Great Depression. They had sent teams of Road Runners to scout every year ranging from 1700 through 2100, mainly flooding the big cities while also scattering teams to check on more rural areas where she might have hidden.

They had no hunch of where they might find her, essentially throwing blindly at a dart board, not even sure if the 400-year span they had covered would be enough. She could have as easily traveled back to the days of dinosaurs and hidden there, but her chances of survival were slim. The plan was to cover the initial 400-year window, completely sweep each year in each state and town, and if nothing turned up, to do it once more before deciding where else to branch out. They also rode the assumption that she would remain in North America.

The Road Runners didn't know if Chris was still providing her protection, or if she had truly ventured out on her own, leaving everyone on edge for that slim chance they'd be the ones to find her. Fortunately, the instructions clearly stated that Commander Briar only wanted to know her location—there was no need to engage with Sonya.

It was a blistering cold night in January of 1933 when a couple of Road Runners spotted Sonya returning home from a trip to the grocery store, two big paper bags clutched in each arm's grip as she walked uphill to her apartment building. She didn't appear to have any sort of security tailing her. They watched for three consecutive days to ensure this fact, and even though she only left her apartment building once a day, all three times for her same route to and from the grocery store, they never spotted another person within fifty feet of her. She lived completely alone, as confirmed when they followed her into the apartment building to find which unit she resided in.

Having a basic feel for her schedule, they wandered around the hallways, stopping to press an ear against her door to see what they could hear. Little did they know, as she blasted the radio for background noise, that she stood on the other side of the door with her pistol cocked and ready to blast whoever might try to break in. Little did they know, she had spotted the two Road Runners tailing her that first night she returned home, and only left in the subsequent days to confirm her suspicions. She was no dummy.

She was the most wanted person in the history of the Road Runners, yet had never committed a crime. While she expected an eventual return to a life on the run, she imagined it would come much later, perhaps after a year or so had passed, not a mere three weeks since fleeing the house in Idaho. Regardless, she was ready, and while she had plans in place to run, she also wanted to fight back this time around. If these same two men kept following her, she'd kill them. Handling her own business had long been her strong suit, and she knew she could handle a pair of Road Runners.

What she didn't know was that Martin had a change of heart. Back in 2020, eighty-seven years ahead of Sonya's current hideout, Martin had packed his bag, stuffing it with clothes, body armor, six different guns, and half a dozen boxes of ammunition. He zipped the bag shut and stared at himself in the mirror hanging on his office wall. "This is it," he told himself.

Two weeks earlier he had officially sworn in his new lieutenant commander, a confident woman by the name of Alina Herrera. Alina had carved a name out for herself running missions across Central America focused on wiping out cartels before they could harm the general public. Her methods were just as savage as the cartels', but she couldn't care less, fighting for justice on every single mission. She also had close ties to their super-agent, Arielle Lucila.

Alina had arrived in Denver and immediately locked herself in her new office, having since been cleared of Gerald's belongings, and remained inside as she crafted a plan to kill Chris Speidel. Martin had worked with numerous teams around the country in regards to the mission of finding and killing Sonya, and he didn't want his new lieutenant to worry about anything else besides Chris.

She lived and breathed her work, her dedication to the organization unlike anyone else Martin had met during his time in the Road Runners. He didn't know it at the time—no one did—but Alina was the perfect fit for this ultimate role.

With the plans brewing and nearing completion for what to do once Sonya was killed, Martin took his packed bag and left his office behind. He had debated delivering some sort of memorable speech to the Denver office, but decided it might sound too much like a farewell. The Council agreed to let him be the one to capture Sonya, while acknowledging his elevated risk of death by going on such a dangerous mission. They only insisted he have a new lieutenant selected in case anything went wrong.

He did as instructed, his heart full with the notion that he would either return a hero, or see his life end once and for all. Both options sounded as equally appeasing for the emotionally torn commander.

Although he didn't concern over his life's outcome on this mission—the Council and Road Runners did, sending ten different guards to accompany him every step of the way. They had strict orders from the Council to not leave his side, regardless of what he directly instructed.

They took two cars to the airport, and all of the guards crammed into the jet with Martin for the quick flight to Chicago. Martin wanted to wait until they landed before taking his swig of Juice to jump back to 1933. His stomach fluttered with nerves as the flight took off into the still afternoon sky, a sense of doom mixed with destiny, practically suffocating his lungs.

Martin looked around the jet to all of the guards there to protect his life, but didn't really *see* them. He felt alone on this mission, knowing these guards were at a high risk of losing their lives should they come anywhere close to Sonya. This was Martin's mission. He had to take his gloves off and get dirty if any of their plans were to proceed.

Per advice from Alina, Martin had worked on playing out the murder scene in his mind. He was able to mentally take a step back and imagine himself killing Sonya, the idea never feeling normal and always tipping him toward a powerful nausea that made his entire body shake. He had to prepare for multiple circumstances, not knowing exactly how it would all play out: knives, guns, bare hands. Whatever it took. She had been ready during the first encounter in 1996 when Strike sent him on this same mission, when he didn't have any intent on actually going through with it.

The stakes were raised now, and everyone knew it. Sonya would be more prepared than ever, expecting Martin to pay a visit. Their initial life together in 1996, when Sonya pulled him deeper into this twisted world, seemed thousands of years in the past. Now he stared into the clouds from his jet's window, the future seemingly endless ahead of him.

For the first time in a while, during these brief moments of reflection, Martin didn't look to the past. All the souls that had touched his life breezed by like the distant memories they were. Izzy, Lela, his mother and father, even his estranged brother who had been the initial spark that started this raging fire, passed through his thoughts without sticking, much like an express train blasting through a station without so much as touching its brakes to slow down.

The flight to Chicago only took a few minutes beyond two hours, and they had landed in no time, the crew of guards remaining in their seats and awaiting instruction. They already knew the plans and each step they'd be taking for the next twenty-four hours, only needing the official call from Martin.

He took a moment to nod to this crew of unfamiliar faces around him. This had seemed a growing trend since becoming commander, as more and more Road Runners entered his life on a daily basis.

Martin pulled the bottle of Juice from his bag that had rested beside his feet during the flight, and unscrewed the cap, raising the bottle to his fellow Road Runners, placing his hand on the jet's wall to ensure the aircraft would come with them during their trip to the past. He tipped it back and took a hard swallow, prompting everyone else to do the same.

After a couple minutes, they had fallen through the usual rumble of the world and woke up in their same positions on the jet, parked at a distant hangar a dozen miles outside of Chicago. The jet's door opened, letting in a brisk gust of cold air that made the cabin's temperature drop fifteen degrees immediately. Martin started for the door and stopped before walking down the steps, admiring the city skyline in the far distance. It was much smaller than what he was used to from his present time, but it appeared majestic nonetheless.

"Welcome to 1933, ladies and gentlemen," he said over his shoulder to the group of guards returning to consciousness. "Let's go."

He stepped out, leading his team into the unknown of the Great Depression, the world silent and still as it only could when destiny loomed.

Martin Briar had regained his sense of purpose as he set out on an adventure that was sure to change his life forever, his only hope that it would also save the world.

Time of Fate

We have one more book to go in the *Wealth of Time* Series! Be sure to pre-order your copy of the epic finale, *Time of Fate*, slated for release in Summer 2021 (please disregard the listed date of December that shows on Amazon). Pre-orders will run at a limited-time discount leading up to release day!

Order HERE - https://www.amazon.com/gp/product/B08RJ9H5S2

GET EXCLUSIVE BONUS STORIES!

Connecting with readers is the best part of this job. Releasing a book into the world is a truly frightening moment every time it happens! Hearing your feedback, whether good or bad, goes a long in shaping future projects and helping me grow as a writer. I also like to take readers behind the scenes on occasion and share what is happening in my wild world of writing. If you're interested, please consider joining my mailing list. If you do so, I'll send you the following as a thank you:

1. A free copy of *Revolution*, a prequel story that goes back in time before Chris Speidel ever knew about the mysterious world of time travel.
2. A free copy of *Road Runners*, a prequel story that visits the origination of the Road Runners organization.

You can get your content **for free,** by signing up HERE.
https://www.andregonzalez.net/Wealth-Of-Time-Bonus

Acknowledgments

Thank you for continuing this wild journey with myself and Martin. Being the second-to-last book of the series, my goal was to set up the story for a strong finish in the sixth book, which I feel was a success. As I write this, I have just finished the first draft for the aforementioned sixth and final book, Time of Fate, which should bring this series to a satisfying end. This is the deepest I've written into a series, and I'm constantly surprised at how much more there is to learn to keep it going—and interesting. Series writing is definitely a unique skillset that I'm glad to have learned since jumping into Wealth of Time.

I wanted to take a moment to thank those who have made this book possible. Stephanie, my editor, for her prompt work and attention to detail. To Dane Low for another beautiful cover, it's becoming harder each time to decide which is my favorite.

Thank you to my Advance Reader team, your feedback is always welcomed and cherished as my final readers before publication day.

To the Dizzy Dragons for the continued support. Even though we've been apart this year due to the pandemic, it still feels like home when we get into our Slack discussions.

And to the ones who keep me driven and motivated each and every day: Arielle, Felix, and Selena. I know you all see how much work is put into this career, I can only hope you'll witness the benefits of it as you grow up.

And lastly, to Natasha, for keeping the faith alive, and sharing the same vision. I couldn't imagine doing this with anyone else.

Andre Gonzalez

2/18/20–01/02/21

Enjoy this book?

You can make a difference!

Reviews are the most helpful tools in getting new readers for any books. I don't have the financial backing of a New York publishing house and can't afford to blast my book on billboards or bus stops.

(Not yet!)

That said, your honest review can go a long way in helping me reach new readers. If you've enjoyed this book, I'd be forever grateful if you could spend a couple minutes leaving it a review (it can be as short as you like) on the Amazon page. You can jump right to the page by clicking below:

US - mybook.to/ZeroHourWOT

UK - mybook.to/ZeroHourWOT

Thank you so much!

Also by Andre Gonzalez

Wealth of Time Series:
Zero Hour (Wealth of Time Series, Book #5)
Keeper of Time (Wealth of Time Series, Book #4)
Bad Faith (Wealth of Time Series, Book #3)
Warm Souls (Wealth of Time Series, Book #2)
Wealth of Time (Wealth of Time Series, Book #1)
Road Runners (Wealth of Time Series, Short Story)
Revolution (Wealth of Time Series, Short Story)

Insanity Series:
The Insanity Series (Books 1-3)
Replicate (Insanity Series, Book #3)
The Burden (Insanity Series, Book #2)
Insanity (Insanity Series, Book #1)
Erased (Insanity Series, Prequel) (Short Story)

The Exalls Attacks:
Followed East (#2)
Followed Home (#1)
A Poisoned Mind (Short Story)

Standalone books:
Resurrection (Amelia Doss Series, Book #1)
Snowball: A Christmas Horror Story

About the Author

Born in Denver, CO, Andre Gonzalez has always had a fascination with horror and the supernatural starting at a young age. He spent many nights wide-eyed and awake, his mind racing with the many images of terror he witnessed in books and movies. Ideas of his own morphed out of movies like *Halloween* and books such as *Pet Sematary* by Stephen King. These thoughts eventually made their way to paper, as he always wrote dark stories for school assignments or just for fun. Followed Home is his debut novel based off of a terrifying dream he had many years ago at the age of 12. His reading and writing of horror stories evolved into a pursuit of a career as an author, where Andre hopes to keep others awake at night with his frightening tales. The world we live in today is filled with horror stories, and he looks forward to capturing the raw emotion of these events, twisting them into new tales, and preserving a legacy in between the crisp bindings of novels.

Andre graduated from Metropolitan State University of Denver with a degree in business in 2011. During his free time, he enjoys baseball, poker, golf, and traveling the world with his family. He believes that seeing the world is the only true way to stretch the imagination by experiencing new cultures and meeting new people.

Andre still lives in Denver with his wife, Natasha, and their three kids.